PRAISE FOR *MAYBE*
WITCHE

"When books are really good we feel like they are speaking directly to us. The ingenious premise behind Jude Atwood's sharp debut *Maybe There Are Witches* is to cast this sensation as an actual spell for young Clara. Her ordinariest of ordinary lives takes a twist toward the darkly fantastic as a newly-discovered book communicates truths about Clara's present it couldn't possibly know and launches her into a harrowing adventure she can't possibly hope to survive. At a time where we all worry our kids might get lost in their phones, *Maybe There Are Witches* poses that they might, instead, get lost in their tomes, and aside from the impending cataclysmic doom they might find within, I can't think of a better fate for young readers like Clara, or yours."

-Steven T. Seagle, co-creator of *Ben 10*, *Big Hero 6*, *Camp Midnight*

"Devotees of supernatural stories reeling from the end of *Stranger Things* reel no longer! Atwood delivers a twisting, turning tale of Midwestern macabre equal parts spine-tingling and laughter-inducing. Teens fighting the doldrums of what can often feel like a charmless world will particularly identify with curious and resilient heroine Clara Hutchins and the town of Biskopskulla that disguises the extraordinary beneath a thin veil of quaint normalcy. Every town is a permeable mirror, a portal of Past and Present, Good and Evil, and Atwood makes Biskopskulla spring to life with the unexpected menace of Bradbury's *Something Wicked This Way Comes* but with a quirkiness and a beating heart all the author's own."

-J.R. Potter, author of *Thomas Creeper and the Gloomsbury Secret*

"Wonderfully plotted with head-spinning twists and turns, I was racing toward the end of this impossible-to-put-down adventure. By turns funny and smart and scary, this book is guaranteed to thrill and enthrall."

-John Calvin Hughes, author of *The Lost Gospel of Darnell Rabren*

Maybe There Are Witches

Jude Atwood

Fitzroy Books

Published by Fitzroy Books
An imprint of
Regal House Publishing, LLC
Raleigh, NC 27605
All rights reserved

https://fitzroybooks.com
Printed in the United States of America

ISBN -13 (paperback): 9781646033645
ISBN -13 (epub): 9781646033652
Library of Congress Control Number: 2022943499

Cover images and design by © C. B. Royal
Author photo by Josh Babich

Regal House Publishing, LLC
https://regalhousepublishing.com

Printed in the United States of America

To Andrea, who often found joy in the scary stuff

1

When Clara woke up Saturday morning, the dolls were staring at her with their cold, lifeless eyes.

Everything *else* about her bedroom in the new house was marvelous. The queen-sized antique bed—with a canopy!—was an elegant place to sleep, and it certainly beat sleeping on a futon in the small apartment she'd shared with her mother before the move. The uneven hardwood floor was a little cold at night, but Clara found an area rug in one of the hallway closets and fixed it in place with double-stick carpet tape.

But there was only one word for the curio cabinet full of antique dolls that once belonged to her grandmother— creepy. Clara vowed to get rid of them as soon as possible.

"Maybe we should keep them," Clara's mother said over grilled cheese sandwiches later that day. "They might have been important to Grandma."

"In that case," Clara said between bites, "you can keep the cabinet in your room. Wait for their little voices to say, 'Come play with us, Ms. Hutchins, and stay with us forever where we never get old…'"

Cecilia Hutchins cocked an eyebrow at her daughter. "All right," she said, with a chuckle. "You can sell them if you promise never to do your doll voice again."

After lunch, the two of them made a list of things that needed to be fixed up in the new place, a colorful Victorian house more than a century old. Its exterior was painted brown, but embellished on all sides with fussy orange and lemon-yellow trim like a chocolate cake decorated by an overzealous cooking-show contestant. The house stood on the corner of Park Street and Mattsson Street, with a patchy lawn dotted with dandelions. The front door, curiously, had been built into the eastern corner of the house, and the walkway leading up to it from the crossroads was a mosaic of cracks. Near the house entrance a massive gray boulder had been positioned next to the walk, protruding four feet or so from the earth. Her mom had tried to move it, but most of its mass appeared to be hidden underground, like a petrified iceberg; even pushing together, they could not budge it an inch. A chiseled inscription in the boulder revealed the house's previous occupation: *Biskopskulla Bed and Breakfast*. "We'll figure out how to move that later," her mother declared. "We've got our hands full with the house for now."

Listing antique dolls on eBay was just one of many projects to be checked off during their first few days. Clara didn't particularly enjoy beating the dust out of the old love seat or heaving a gargantuan 1975 Electrolux vacuum across the floor, but these tasks kept her busy and kept her mind off a looming event she was absolutely dreading—the first day of school.

Her grandmother had died earlier that summer, a week before her thirteenth birthday. Clara felt sad, not because she'd known her grandmother well, but because she'd barely known her at all. And now, of course, she never would. Clara's mother hadn't gotten along well with her own mother—Catherine Hutchins, the late owner of the only bed and breakfast in Biskopskulla, Illinois—so Clara, as a result, hadn't seen her grandmother in years.

Clara tried not to think about how much she was going to miss California, but she couldn't blame her mother for moving back to Illinois, even though they'd *already moved* just one year ago, from one part of Orange County to another. They'd inherited this house and all of its contents, the parcel of land on which it stood, and a small amount of life insurance money—enough to pay the property taxes for a year or two. There was still no way they could afford real estate in the expensive Southern California market, but they were now homeowners in tiny Biskopskulla, a town that boasted all of 140 residents!

Biskopskulla. Even the town's name sounded unpleasant. But it was home now, and Clara was determined to make the best of things, even though the last move hadn't been easy.

The last time she started at a new school, she didn't even talk to anyone for the first two months, and once she felt ready to (barely) acknowledge her new classmates, they already had plenty of practice ignoring her. For the entire year, her mom kept encouraging her to *make a fresh start*, but Clara just withdrew—and grew more miserable.

She was determined not to let that happen again in Biskopskulla! This was a new home...even if it didn't feel like it yet.

Much of the house had an intricate museum quality, with ornate light fixtures and imposing door frames, but the basement was just a huge one-room storage space, crammed with years' worth of stuff. Thus, all of Sunday was devoted to cleaning out the basement, to turn it into a rec room. Clara wanted to keep herself as busy as possible; it was the only way she could think of to stave off the terror of tomorrow, when she would start, yet again, at a new school where she wouldn't know a single person.

At the bottom of the stairs, she picked up an old hobbyhorse. Leg broken beyond repair? Into the TRASH box. An ancient sewing machine? Best to assume a collector might want it. Into the SELL box. A pair of orange bowling shoes? Clearly items to DONATE.

As she organized, another pile developed of things Clara wanted to keep for herself—a pincushion shaped like a tomato, a quill pen, and a snow globe with a tiny Victorian street scene.

Once the basement's concrete floor was cleared, she swept it, and then swept again.

If I'm going to do this, I might as well do it right, she

thought, and filled a bucket with hot soapy water. She took a sponge from under the kitchen sink and carefully scrubbed from one corner of the floor to another. Along the center of one wall, she discovered, was a rectangular patch of brick inlaid within the concrete flooring. The grooves between the bricks were filthy, and Clara scrubbed so hard that her elbow caught the water bucket and knocked it over.

"Oh no!" Clara exclaimed, grabbing a towel to mop up the mess. Then she noticed something curious—bubbles were emerging along a crack in the base of the wall, right where the water pooled. As she attempted to soak up the water, wondering what these bubbles might mean, a portion of mortar from the wall started to crumble under her towel. Curious, she pulled away the mortar to reveal a dark arched hole. A recess for a fireplace that had been closed in, she realized. Of course! That explained the brick flooring right in front of it. Peering inside the hole in the wall, there was just enough light to see something on the floor of the fireplace, where logs might once have been.

Clara reached in to pull out a small wooden box, thick with dust. She blew off the dust and tried to figure out how to open it.

An hour later, she was still trying.

Clara sighed. The box was impenetrable. Rectangular in shape, it appeared to have moving pieces cut into the sides. When she pressed on a recessed panel, it would give, ever so slightly. But she couldn't find a hinge or a keyhole, or anything else to suggest the box might open in a conventional way. Every panel that looked like it might slide or swing open was blocked by another part of the box.

It's a puzzle, she thought. *It's an old-fashioned toy.* Holding it up to her ear, she shook it, gently. There was definitely something solid moving around inside. The box must open by some trick, Clara thought, without a key or a lid, without pressing, pulling, or sliding any particular panel—for she had tried all of that.

She ruled out burning the box or submerging it in water—that might damage whatever was inside.

What if the lock could be triggered by gravity? she mused. What if she dropped it? Or threw it up in the air? Perhaps it was possible to build a box that could only open in the moment of seeming weightlessness when it was thrown into the air but before it started to fall back down?

She threw the box into the air, once, twice, a third time.

On the third try, the box spun as it left her grasp and she heard three quick clicks.

Aha! Was that the answer—spinning it?

She placed the box on the concrete floor and spun it, fast. Again she heard a click. The top panel of the box wiggled, ever so slightly, and Clara was sure she was on the right track. Spinning the box again resulted in a second, louder click, and Clara was finally able to gently pull the top panel from the box.

Inside was an old book bound in tattered black leather that was warped with age.

She took the book out of the box and opened it carefully. The endpaper, mottled with mold, was of an ornate vintage design decorated with leaves and flowers. The thick, yellowed pages were stuck together—possibly due to the same water damage that had warped the cover and left mold on the endpaper.

Clara took one of the pins from the tomato-shaped pincushion and carefully inserted it between the first and second pages, sliding it all the way around until the pages were free. Holding her breath with excitement, she turned the first page to reveal a delicate spidery script.

A Collection of Thoughts by Constance Love. August 2, 1867.

The next line made the hair on the back of Clara's neck stand up and goosebumps rise on her arms.

For Clara.

2

By the next morning, Clara had convinced herself that the book's dedication was just a coincidence. Clara was not an uncommon name, after all. She'd managed to reveal the first four pages of the book, but the rest seemed so firmly stuck together that even her pin could not unstick them. Reluctant to damage the book, she had not investigated further. Clearly, it was an old diary that belonged to someone called Constance Love.

The first entry, after that startling dedication, presented a question:

Does every person feel as if he has so many thoughts in his head that he must write them down or be overwhelmed?

I cannot know. But I know that I must write down the thoughts I am thinking. If you are reading this, I say, good day, and do not judge me too severely.

This entry was followed by a page of pressed flowers, with names like *Nodding Onion* and *Thimbleweed*. After this came... recipes. There was a recipe for buckwheat cakes, underneath which was a curious inscription: *I had a vision that these would taste better if I added salt to the mix. My vision proved true.* And, an even curiouser comment: *My visions always prove true.*

There wasn't time to dwell on this strange discovery. For better or worse, Clara started at her new school today.

Her mother made a big celebratory breakfast of eggs, bacon, oatmeal, and—

"Mom, what's this?" Clara asked, holding up a syrup-drenched forkful.

"Do you like those? It's a new recipe I found online. Buckwheat pancakes."

Clara swallowed. *Coincidence.*

"You'd better head out, hon. You don't want to be late on the first day."

After breakfast, Clara said goodbye to her mother, shrugged on her backpack, and headed out the front door.

She had never been able to *walk* to any school before, and she seldom ate a big breakfast. Her belly full of food, Clara felt rather like the granite boulder outside her house. It would be good to walk it all off a bit, she thought, as she set off down the road.

She passed a number of old brick houses behind large grassy lawns, then crossed over Main Street, past a post office and an antique store, until she got to the edge of town where Prairie Dale Middle School was located. Even if she had been uncertain of the way, the vehicles in the parking lot would have given her a clue. Students from a number of small towns rode old black-and-yellow school buses to this, the only middle school in the region.

She followed her classmates through the parking lot toward the double glass doors of a sprawling one-story building. Glancing up, she witnessed a curious sight—hundreds of birds of different species perched on the slanting edge of the school's roof. When a screeching car alarm sounded in the faculty parking lot, all but one took off in a flutter of wings. The remaining bird, its feathers so black they looked iridescent, cocked its head to the side, its beady eyes fixed upon Clara as she walked through the doors on her way to her first class.

She didn't notice.

Clara had PE first period, which consisted mostly of tests of physical ability. The students stretched and did crunches. Then they did push-ups, then pull-ups—Clara managed two, and felt proud of this—and other physical feats, all dutifully recorded in a big red book by a bored-looking teacher. The final task of the day was a timed run, four laps around the gym, and a red-haired girl with braces gave Clara the first advice she received at the new school. "Don't go too fast," she whispered, as if the CIA were listening. "They grade you on how much you improve at the end of the semester. There's no reason to get a good time on the first day. It's *farcical*."

In between classes, Clara felt horribly nervous. Other girls, she noticed, laughed and chatted with friends they'd been spending time with over the summer, and hugged the friends they hadn't seen in a while. But none of them seemed particularly interested in the new girl.

Clara's second class wasn't really a class at all: study hall.

"Okay, guys and girls," said Mr. Simons, the stout business teacher who was in charge of second-period study hall. "Let's get one thing straight. You are here to study. You are not here to talk. That means you do homework. That means you read. That means you do not disturb each other, and you do not take your cell phones out."

Clara didn't recognize anyone from her PE class. What was the point of having study hall immediately after gym class? she wondered. Why couldn't the first day be a Let's-Get-To-Know-Each-Other day instead of an hour of total silence? Everyone else seemed to have something to work on.

"There are four library passes," Mr. Simons continued. "If you need a book, or you need to look something up, you come up and get a pass from me, you go to the library, then you bring the pass back when you're done," Mr. Simons continued. "Also, since it's the first day, I need a volunteer to be a library worker for this semester."

Without thinking, Clara raised her hand She didn't know what library workers did, but it couldn't be worse than sitting in a silent room with nothing to do.

Clara followed Mr. Simons's directions to the library, a room that looked much like every school library she had been in before, with tightly packed shelves of books and a large desk, over which hung a sign that read Media and Special Reserves.

"Who have we here?" a tall lady boomed, taking Clara by surprise. Clearly the librarian, she wore a knee-length floral dress, a red cardigan, and flat black shoes that looked impossibly wide.

"I'm Clara. I'm new," she said, as if to explain her own existence.

"Well, well, welcome! I'm Mrs. Maynard, spelled with a Y," she said, with a grin, as if inviting Clara to join her in appreciating the quirks of silent letters.

"I just don't know if I could trust a letter that is only *sometimes* a vowel," Clara ventured, frowning.

Mrs. Maynard's eyes widened, and Clara hoped she hadn't sounded disrespectful. But then the older woman broke into a cackle. "I should have thought of that before I got married."

It took Clara a second to realize that, of course, Mrs. Maynard hadn't always been Mrs. Maynard.

The librarian pulled up a chair for Clara to join her at the checkout desk. She wanted to know what it was like to move from California to Illinois. Did Clara know anyone in town? Who was her favorite author? Did she play any sports?

The answers were: Not really. Charlotte Brontë. And, no.

Mrs. Maynard also explained the duties of a library helper, which, unsurprisingly, mostly involved checking books out and checking them back in. At the end of the hour, the bell rang, and Clara stood to leave.

"Clara," Mrs. Maynard began, "we have scholastic bowl team practice in the library on Thursdays after school. We need one more person, and I think you would really like it. Would you be willing to give it a try? It might be a nice way to meet some other students. But be sure to wear rubber-soled shoes, just in case!"

Rubber-soled shoes?

Clara's classes the rest of the day consisted of English, pre-algebra, life science, American history, and art.

The red-haired girl from Clara's PE class was also in her American history class. She raised her hand often, so Clara quickly learned that her name was Kaitlyn, and she talked like a vocabulary worksheet and was particularly fond of *farcical*. The Boston Tea Party was *farcical*. The syllabus policy on late assignments—none were accepted for any reason—was *totally farcical*.

Her history teacher, Mr. Froehlich, had a mop of silver-gray hair and tended to interrupt himself a lot. The student chairs took up only half of the classroom; the rear half seemed to function as a supply closet. Clara's attention was drawn, however, to a large-scale model of a town encased in plexiglass. It was Biskopskulla, she realized, spotting the steeple of the town church, a bright red building that looked like an old school, and even the Biskopskulla Bed and Breakfast! The buildings, though brightly colored, seemed as if they had been built quite some time ago. The green felt that lay underneath, representing grass, was faded and yellowed at the edges, and the plexiglass case was slightly opaque with age.

Clara thought about the school she'd attended the year before, and how unhappy she'd been. She felt a little sick. She resolved to strike up a conversation with someone before the end of the day.

In Mr. Hawthorne's art classroom, students sat at long tables around the perimeter of the room, facing the center. Shelves of art supplies lined the walls: canvas, paper, and cloth. Clear plastic drawers held acrylics and watercolors, and jars accommodated different sizes of paintbrushes.

Mr. Hawthorne began the class by announcing that every student was expected to turn in at least four projects at the end of the semester, but they could work on as many as they wanted over the next eighteen weeks and choose their four favorites. "If you need some ideas," he said, "feel free to look through the books and magazines at the back of the classroom."

Clara didn't consider herself much of an artist, but once in summer camp she'd helped paint a mural celebrating female scientists. She imagined she could figure out some kind of interesting project to occupy her time.

Some classmates knew immediately what they wanted to do. One student in a Velvet Underground T-shirt, with long blond hair, took a sketchbook out of a backpack and scrawled a few notes before standing up to show Mr. Hawthorne. "That looks fine, Chris," Mr. Hawthorne said, nodding his approval.

Clara leafed through the art magazines and nature books featuring birds or barns of Illinois.

"If you paint a barn, I will never be your friend."

A wiry boy with brown eyes and a shock of black hair was smirking at her, and Clara couldn't tell if he was being mean or friendly.

"I don't think I'll paint a barn. I don't think it would fit in the classroom," she replied.

He grinned. "In Hawthorne's class, there are really only three options. All any of us make is something weird, something beautiful, or something tacky. Barns are the ultimate in tacky."

Clara decided that she would pretend he was being friendly, even if he wasn't. It was nice to have someone talking to her. "Which path are you going to take?" she asked.

"I do paintings of insects at extreme magnification."

"That sounds weird."

"It's beautiful."

"Oh. I see."

"Don't worry," he said. "I can understand the mistake."

Clara picked up another book with four black and white

woodcut illustrations on the cover. *A Brief History of the Village of Biskopskulla*. One image showed a group of people in old-fashioned clothes building a church. Another depicted a man laid out on a table in front of a crowd of people. The third was of a woman with a noose around her neck standing on a chair under a tree. And the fourth showed a man with dynamite in his hands running out of a burning tavern.

"This town has a violent history," Clara said.

"Yeah," the boy agreed, with pride in his voice. "It's awesome." He pointed at the woman with the noose. "She was one of the last people killed for witchcraft in the whole state, possibly in the whole country."

"That's cool, I guess." Clara didn't really share his enthusiasm for the macabre.

"Yeah! Her family still lived here until just recently. It was big news for people who are into history and creepy stuff. Constance Love's bloodline dies out in Biskopskulla!"

"Constance Love?" Clara asked, startled. "That was her name?"

That was the name on the first page of the book she had discovered in her basement. *A Collection of Thoughts by Constance Love*.

"Yeah. She was hanged in the 1870s for being a witch. Her great-granddaughter used to own the bed and breakfast on the corner of Mattsson and Park, but she died over the summer."

Was he messing with her?

"Really? The woman who owned the bed and breakfast was related to the witch?"

"For sure!" the boy said. "I mean, it's a complicated family, but she was her great-grandmother."

Clara shook her head, annoyed that her mother had never mentioned this alarming bit of family history.

"What's your name? I'm, uh, Clara."

"A Clara? I've never met a person with an article for a first name."

Clara chose not to acknowledge this. Too silly.

"I'm Gary," he said. "So what brought you to Biskopskul-la? Is it just the fact that it's northwestern Illinois's seven-teenth-most-popular tourist destination?"

"I live in that bed and breakfast now," Clara told him. "The woman who used to own it, the woman who died last summer? She was my grandmother."

"Your actual blood-related grandmother?"

"Uh-huh."

"That is so cool!" Gary blurted out. "Oh, hey, I'm really sorry about your grandma," he added. "So I guess Constance Love's bloodline didn't die out after all! Wow."

Gary looked at her and narrowed his eyes which would have made her uncomfortable even if she didn't already know that he was a guy who a) liked to draw giant insects and b) had a morbid fascination with her dead relative from long ago.

"Clara, you've got witch's blood in you."

The bell rang. Clara had never learned quite so much on the first day of school.

3

Clara asked Mr. Hawthorne if she could take the *Brief History* book home. She was intrigued to learn more about Biskopskulla. She'd seen references to this tiny town's history here and there. There were plaques on half of the buildings and the town square was called the "historic district," but it hadn't occurred to her to wonder what it was like for the people who lived and died in these buildings and on these streets.

This place sure seemed to have an unusual history.

The town of Biskopskulla was supposed to be utopia. It was founded by Erik Mattsson, a prophet who, for a bad-tempered old man, had a surprising number of devoted followers. When Mattsson arrived in the United States with a group of Swedish immigrants more than one hundred and sixty years ago, they decided that northwestern Illinois was the right place to build a perfect society. If you travel to Illinois during late summer, you might think the same thing.

After one-fifth of the settlement died of cholera during the first winter, they began to have second thoughts, but they were committed too deeply to back out. Erik Mattsson also made it difficult for anyone to withdraw, since everything the colonists owned was considered to be colony property. If you wanted to leave, you left with nothing.

In the wake of that first harsh winter, the colony at Biskopskulla was very successful. Duties—like farming, carpentry, baking, and textile work—were split between colonists, and everyone had enough to live comfortably. The number of buildings and houses grew from zero to several dozen, and people started families. The children of Biskopskulla had never seen their parents' homeland of Sweden, and many of them did not speak Swedish. Mandatory church services were held every day, and they lasted about three hours—and even longer on Sunday.

By all accounts, Erik Mattsson was a smart and charismatic man. People who got to know him well felt that he knew what he was talking about, and they trusted him, even when he suggested that he was the new messiah.

Unfortunately, Erik Mattsson was shot at close quarters by a man who had not taken the time to get to know him, and who did not believe he was a new messiah at all. Charles Worth, a farmer from a neighboring town, married a young woman from the colony and built a house for her on the edge of Biskopskulla. When Worth decided to move to Chicago to go into business with his cousin, Erik Mattsson and his followers (they would be called Mattssonists in history books, but they did not use that term for themselves) insisted, per the colony rule, that everything the Worths owned was community property, and that it must be left behind. Charles Worth objected, and he was run out of town.

None of this sat well with Mr. Worth, and he showed up at the colony church on a bright November Sunday morning. Charles Worth shot Erik Mattsson in the chest in front of hundreds of his followers and then escaped back to Chicago.

What happened next brought about the end of the Mattssonists' religion. Although Erik Mattsson died almost immediately after being shot, he had spoken many times in the past of his own resurrection. The colonists cleaned his wound, dressed him in his finest clothes, laid him out on a table at the front of the church, and waited for him to rise again.

On the first day, nothing happened. A few of the colonists—the ones who had always been a little skeptical—began to fear that their prophet might have been mistaken. After the third day, the body began to smell, and on the fourth day, some of the more prominent residents of the colony decided they had better bury him.

Three days later, Constance Love was born to a young couple in Biskopskulla. She was the second of two daughters.

People began moving in and out of the colony more freely, and within three years, the town of Biskopskulla was just another prairie town, where individual farmers and craftsmen traded with each other. Some people grew wealthier, and some people grew poorer. Townspeople still went to church, and they were still devoutly religious, but they slowly stopped mentioning Erik Mattsson and his radical beliefs to one another.

By the time Constance Love was a teenage girl, the prophet Erik Mattsson was nothing but a distant memory.

She attended school in the colony schoolhouse where all grade levels studied in the same room. She seldom misbehaved, except that she sometimes would stand up in the middle of lessons and run home to help care for her ailing mother. She seemed to just *know* when she was needed at home.

After her mother died, she never left class early again.

4

Clara wanted to read more of the secret book she'd found in the basement, but she had *so* much homework. At school, during art class, her new friend Gary complained about the town—it was too small, the school was too cliquey, nothing ever happened.

He talked so much that Mr. Hawthorne, who seldom said anything, chastised him. "Mr. Mahler? You getting any work done over there?"

Unlike most of the other students, whose lives seemed so complete that they didn't need a new friend, Gary seemed to be so desperately bored that a student like Clara, the new girl from California, was much more interesting to him than his long-time classmates. He also had difficulty talking for any length of time without insulting someone, which contributed, as Kaitlyn might say, to his *dearth* of friends. Chris, the long-haired boy Clara had dubbed Velvet Underground, also sat at their table during art.

"What are you guys doing this weekend?" he asked. "My oldest brother gets out this weekend so we're all having a big dinner."

"I'm definitely busy," Gary offered.

"I'm doing homework," Clara contributed, thinking of the book in her basement. She was determined to spend some time that weekend reading more of that strange book, especially now that she had learned more about the history of Biskopskulla. After class, Gary said, "Not to be weird, but my mom really wants me to invite some friends over for dinner. Do you like Vietnamese food?"

Clara hadn't eaten Vietnamese food since she left Orange County. "I have to ask my mom," she said. Her mother would be thrilled she was making friends already, she knew.

"What did Chris mean about his brother getting out?" Clara asked.

"Chris's brother has been in jail for, like, a year. Chris has three older brothers and they've all been to jail. But Chris never even gets detention at school. He's like the white sheep of the family."

Gary Mahler's house, a pretty yellow house with a neatly trimmed lawn, was at 26 Flower Street and only a fifteen-minute walk from Clara's house. She knocked on the front door, a bit nervous about making a good impression.

A trim Asian woman in jeans and a sweater opened the door. "Hello!" she sang out with a warm smile, her dark eyes twinkling. "You must be Clara!" she said. "I am so happy to meet you. Come on inside. Is it cold out?"

It wasn't cold yet, really, but Clara felt a sharpness in the air that suggested the outside air was about to become very cold indeed.

After a delicious dinner of *cha ca*—a fried fish dish with garlic and ginger—and *nem ran*, crunchy spring rolls, Clara, Gary, and Mrs. Mahler sat together in the den. Mr. Mahler had work to do, and after saying goodbye to Clara he retreated to his home office. The den was more of a library, really, and was lined with floor-to-ceiling bookcases that covered three of the four walls. A chair and sofa were upholstered in deep red, and several lamps cast warm, yellow pools of light.

"So you're from Orange County?" Mrs. Mahler asked Clara enthusiastically as she settled into the chair with her coffee. "You must miss the shopping. We don't have a single decent mall here. If I really want options, I have to go to Chicago—a three-hour drive!"

"Well, my mom hates shopping and long car drives, so I don't think we'll be going to Chicago anytime soon. She always says you're a hundred times more likely to die in a car than in a plane or train."

At this, there was a sudden silence, which was just starting to get awkward when Mrs. Mahler said, brightly, "Well, would you kids like hot chocolate?"

"Sure, Mom," Gary said.

After his mother disappeared into the kitchen, he told Clara that his parents' first son, his older brother, died in a car accident before Gary was born. "I guess my mom was really depressed for a long time," he said. "And then they decided the best thing to do would be to have another kid."

Clara struggled to figure out what to say. "That's horrible. I'm so, so sorry."

"It's okay. I mean, I never met my brother. A rabbit ran out onto the road ahead of him and he swerved to avoid it and he lost control. Just a moment of kindness for a stupid *rabbit*, and it was all over.

"That's terrible."

"Sometimes the mood around here gets a little weird, but every family has weird stuff, I guess."

"I should never have said that thing about dying in a car crash. Should I go apologize to your mom?" she asked, feeling guilty.

Gary looked at her for a moment. Finally he said, "No. It's not a big deal. It's not like you said something that wasn't true. People get used to that sort of thing." He looked thoughtful. "You know what you *should* do? Ask my mom about the witch."

He pointed toward one of the bookshelves behind him. Clara went over to look more closely at the titles on the spines.

Encyclopedia of American Witchcraft and *Biskopskulla: The Utopia on the Prairie*.

"Wow, your mom is really into witches, huh?" she asked.

"It's Mom's hobby," Gary said. "She's an expert on occult history and local lore." He pointed to a glass-fronted cabinet, where the books within, with mottled black covers, were clearly far older than the rest. "A couple of those books are a hundred years old. She buys them online."

"Wow," Clara said again.

It turned out that Mrs. Mahler was such an expert on the town's history that she worked as a paid tour guide on weekends in the summer. Her most popular tour, Ghosts of Old Biskopskulla, started at the village hall and included all the historic buildings of their small town. Mrs. Mahler entertained the tourists with stories of terrible things that had happened and the spirits who were said to haunt the premises.

"Clara, your family has a rich history in this town. And this is one of the most haunted towns in North America, did you know that? Of course, there is no such thing as ghosts, but don't tell the tourists that or business might dry up!" She laughed. "They're just stories. I have to keep reminding this one"—she gestured toward Gary—"because he and his father lack my healthy skepticism."

"Mom," Gary said. "The bookcase moved. I saw it."

"Gary," she said affectionately, ruffling his hair, "it's no use. You can't join the ghost tour as a guide until you're sixteen. Nice try, though."

She unfolded a copy of an old map of Biskopskulla and pointed to the northeastern part of it.

"This might interest you, Clara. Our house is here in this section. They didn't bother to draw every single house in town. Your house, however, gets special treatment." Her finger pointed at a tiny drawing of the Biskopskulla Bed and Breakfast in the lower left corner of the map.

Then Mrs. Mahler told a colorful version of the story of Erik Mattsson and his eventual failure to rise from the dead.

"On some nights, however, people still say they hear Erik Mattsson walking the floors of the old church house, preparing to kick all the nonbelievers out of town," Mrs. Mahler added.

"Not really," Gary added.

"No, definitely not," his mother agreed, with a grin. "I've never heard anyone say that. But this is the script the tourism committee approved."

She proceeded to explain the colorful characters of the town, where they had lived and where they had died, pointing out the locations on the old map.

Constance Love was clearly the star attraction of the Ghosts of Old Biskopskulla tour. She was, said Mrs. Mahler, accused of being a wicked woman who used witchcraft to make men feeble and make women sick. Townsfolk claimed that she caused pregnancies to end in stillbirth, crops to die, and cows' milk to dry up.

"After her trial, she was hanged from a tree, somewhere outside of town," Mrs. Mahler said.

"Where outside of town?" Clara asked in a whisper, fascinated.

"Nobody knows exactly where," Mrs. Mahler replied. "And, of course, her trial was not a real trial, not as we understand them to be today, with a real judge. The courthouse around here wasn't built until years later. The whole affair was unusual, because there hadn't been any witch hunts in Illinois for more than a century, and as far as we know, there hasn't been one since."

"Did Constance Love ever live in my house?" Clara asked, curious.

"That's an excellent question. The village doesn't have a record of that. But it's a very old house, and we know that it's been in the family for more than a century. Even after Constance Love was killed, the town saw its share of tragedy. Have you heard about Hawley Douglas? He was a prohibitionist, who blew up two basement saloons in town in 1909. He also tried to blow up the village church, but the wick on the dynamite only burned a little and then went out. Villagers at the time saw the hand of God in this—they thought that God had intervened to save the church but allowed the wicked saloons to be destroyed."

"What happened to him?" Clara asked, entranced.

"Well, Hawley thought the saloons were empty, but Thomas Thorpe, owner of one of the establishments, was sleeping in a room above the saloon and was killed. Hawley Douglas was tried for murder and found not guilty by reason of insanity. He lived out the rest of his days at the Illinois Asylum for the Incurably Insane—"

"That's a real place," Gary interrupted, excitedly. "It's in Peoria. The Illinois Asylum for the Incurably Insane. It sounds fake, doesn't it?"

Clara agreed.

"We're going there someday. Mom loves creepy old haunted places, don't you, Mom?"

"As long as they start giving tours again. I'm too old to go sneaking into old buildings," she said with a smile. "Oh, by the way, Clara, do you run?"

"When I'm…chased?" Clara replied hesitantly, unsure of what Mrs. Mahler was asking.

"No, she means for exercise," Gary clarified. "There's a race in town this month. Mom and I are going to be running it. The Hawley Douglas Crazy Bomber 5k Run. It started a few years ago as a fundraiser. People come from all around the area. You should join us. Maybe your mom too?"

"I've really never run a race before. Would I have to start training?"

"Oh, it's a 5k," Gary said. "That's like three miles. It's not a big deal."

Running three miles did not sound fun to Clara, but she promised to think about it.

After the kids had finished their hot chocolates and Mrs. Mahler's coffee had been drained to the dregs, Gary's mother insisted upon driving Clara home. "It's dark, and I'd like to meet your mother," she said. "Besides that, the most recent ghost sightings in Biskopskulla have been from the past year." she added with a mischievous grin. "A woman in black has been seen walking beside the road. When motorists stop to ask if she needs help, she disappears."

"Is that true?" Clara asked.

Mrs. Mahler just shrugged. "Well, if we see a woman in black on the way to your house, we'll just keep driving." She smiled sweetly. "But there's no such thing as ghosts."

5

During Tuesday's art class, Clara began her new project. She'd decided to make a watercolor painting of her house, the former Biskopskulla Bed and Breakfast.

She found a black-and-white photo of the house in the Biskopskulla history book. Although the photo was dated 1930, the house looked much the same—the front door set at an angle in the corner, the covered porch wrapping around the sides, even the big boulder positioned next to the sidewalk.

She sat next to Chris and across the table from Gary.

"So what are you guys working on?" Chris asked.

"I'm doing a watercolor painting of the house I moved into," Clara showed him.

"Sweetness!" Chris exclaimed. "Yeah, I heard you moved into the Death & Dinner."

"You mean, the Bed & Breakfast, right?" Clara replied.

"Yeah. Same thing—just a different time of life and day, you know?"

Gary snickered.

"I live out by the refuse heap," Chris offered, selecting pencils from a plastic container on the table.

"The town junkyard," Gary added helpfully.

"What happened to your hand, Chris?" Clara pointed toward a bandage that wrapped around Chris's left forearm. "Yeah," he said with a lopsided grin. "I was practicing fire-spinning and I had it going good but I got the wick too close to my arm and I burned myself."

Clara's eyes widened. "Oh my gosh!"

Chris nodded. "Yeah, it was pretty awesome."

The conversation went like that for the rest of the period. Chris told them all about his knife collection, his ninja training, and his inventions, fashioned out of rusted car bits and other things he had salvaged from the junkyard. As she left art class, Clara couldn't help but feel that Chris's hobbies made her own interests seem boring indeed.

That afternoon was the first day of scholastic bowl practice, and Clara forced herself to attend. Gary was reading a magazine at the periodicals desk when she entered, making her way over to Mrs. Maynard's desk.

"Dude," he said to her, which seemed to be an odd way to address a girl. "I thought he'd never shut up. Are you joining the scholastic bowl team? Are you super smart?"

Clara didn't know how to answer a question like that. "I'm…okay, I guess. I read a lot."

"Well-read. Got it. That's good. Jason Carlyle graduated last year, and he was our literature guy."

Mrs. Maynard arrived with Kaitlyn and two boys she hadn't met before. One was Myron, who was tall and pale, with dark hair and thick, dark eyebrows. The other was Edison, a foreign-exchange student from Ecuador.

Myron spoke aloud to himself in a way that Clara found odd. When Mrs. Maynard explained how practice would proceed, he said, to nobody in particular, "I think I have this. Do I have this? I have it."

A team, Clara gathered, consisted of at least five students representing a school. And while only five students could compete at a time, teams with more than five participants could substitute members in and out during the break halfway through every match.

The competition itself was run like a game show. Teams from two schools sat at tables next to each other, and each student held an electric buzzer in their hand. ("Did everyone wear rubber-soled shoes?" Mrs. Maynard had asked at the beginning of practice, and Clara honestly couldn't tell if she was kidding or if she really thought there was a risk of electric shock.) A moderator faced the two teams and read toss-up questions out loud, one at a time. If you knew the answer to a toss-up question, you needed to buzz in before you were allowed to say anything. Once you were recognized by the moderator, you could answer the question. If you were correct, you earned ten points. After a team answered a toss-up question correctly, a set of questions would be read—the multi-part bonus questions. Teams had up to thirty seconds to work on scratch paper and discuss the bonus questions. After that, the captain, or a person designated by the captain, would answer the bonus. If your team got the bonus question wrong, the other team had the opportunity to answer, but they didn't get any extra time.

It seemed a little strange to Clara, but fun nonetheless. She liked watching quiz shows on TV, but it had never occurred to her that she might compete in one at school.

For practice, Mrs. Maynard read questions and the students buzzed in and answered. The questions were divided up among subject areas: science, literature, social studies, and math, plus occasional questions about fine arts or miscellaneous topics. Gary knew a lot about history, and he had clearly read a lot of books. Kaitlyn had a pretty big vocabulary, and she knew a fair amount about biology, but not much about chemistry or physics. Edison knew a great deal about geography and current events and Myron buzzed in whenever a question about sports came up.

After practice, Clara lingered with Kaitlyn, who was waiting for her stepmother to pick her up.

"So you're from California, huh?" she asked.

Clara nodded.

"Must be nice. All those movie stars and beaches."

"Well, I miss the beaches, but I didn't actually see too many movie stars on a day-to-day basis."

Kaitlyn nodded, as if to say, *Darn those pesky movie stars.* "I'd love to go there someday. This part of Illinois has a *paucity* of excitement."

"Well, I'm looking forward to snow."

Kaitlyn folded her hands. "Snow is awesome—for the first three days. Then it gets old."

When Kaitlyn got a text message from her stepmother in the parking lot, she offered Clara a ride home. Clara declined but regretted the decision ten minutes later when it started to rain.

6

Guess what!" Clara's mom asked when she got home. "Um, you got a job?" Clara asked.

"Hon, you are getting way too good at this game. Yeah, I got a job. With benefits."

"Would this be the hospital job you were talking about last week? Or are you going to be night watchwoman at a creepy doll factory?"

"Hospital job. Medical receptionist, but I'll also be learning to do medical billing, which means I could get a raise in the next year."

"Congratulations, Mom. They're gonna love you."

"The only problem, Clare, is that I have to work second shift two nights a week for the first few months. That means I'll be out until midnight, maybe until one in the morning. Do you think you can handle yourself? I'll try to make sure it's on school nights, so you'll of course be going to bed early and you won't even miss me."

"Mom, in medieval times, girls my age were married and raising children of their own. I think I can manage a dinner or two by myself."

"Thanks, kiddo," Clara's mom kissed the top of her head, "and don't even think about getting married for years and years."

The next night, while her mother was at work, Clara decided to take advantage of the opportunity to read more of the mysterious book she'd discovered in the basement. She washed her hands carefully, then dried them thoroughly before touching the brittle paper. Using a knife to unstick the pages made her a little nervous—she worried about accidentally ripping up the text. Proceeding carefully, she managed to pry apart two more pages.

Dear girl, the next page began, *I have much to tell you.*

Clara was unnerved again by the sensation that this book seemed to be addressing her directly.

I have been ill with fever, and in my fever, I had the most profound visions. I had a vision of you, too. A pretty girl, dressed most strangely. Taller than me. Your hair is shorter than the girls I know. You read under a single bright lantern. Soon, the shadows will be moving.

Clara's finger paused before turning the next page, a shiver running up her spine. She talked aloud to herself, to make the room less silent. "I'm not *that* pretty. And…any time you imagine what a person in the future will look like, you'll picture them dressed strangely."

She looked up at the bare light bulb hanging from the ceiling. "And that's not a lantern. When was the light bulb invented, anyway?"

She heard a distant siren that steadily grew louder—was it a fire truck?—until it rattled the foundations of the house as it drove past. Clara had a fleeting thought, hoping that that nobody was hurt, and then—

Ordinarily, what happened next wouldn't have bothered her. The light bulb was swaying back and forth because a heavy truck drove past the house. It made sense, then, didn't it, that the shadows throughout the room were, in fact, moving back and forth?

Clara looked down at the book, suddenly afraid to keep reading.

But a part of her was afraid to *stop* reading.

The next several pages turned out to contain a list of descriptions of the weather. Each one was dated—beginning with April 19, 1868—and most descriptions contained just one or two words. *Sunshine*, or *Rain*, or *Terrible fog that lifts by noon*. The handwriting on these pages was even smaller than before, and Clara tried at first to carefully decipher every word. Then she got bored and decided to skip ahead and see what other secrets the book held.

She chose a spot more than halfway through the book and inserted the knife blade between two pages. When she finally got them apart, she opened the book to reveal blank pages.

Another spot, earlier in the book, was also blank. Then, upon separating pages near the end of the book, she found a brief journal entry.

Dear girl, don't be foolish. Books are read from the front to the back.

That made the hairs on the back of Clara's neck stand up. Could this be real? she wondered. Unnerved, she took a deep breath and vowed to keep reading.

From the front of the book, she decided.

There were a few more pages of weather descriptions, all written in the same tight flowery script.

Then one page contained two columns, letters and numbers, under the heading *Unnatural Calamities.*

DG 5

FM 19

SC 12

BT 21

What did it mean?

She read on. On the next few pages, Constance wrote about her life, her mother, Margreta; her sister, Mary; and the little house they lived in on the outskirts of Biskopskulla.

Margreta was often ill, and Constance and Mary took turns taking care of her. Their father had died when she was young, and he'd left the family many books that Constance used to read to her mother.

At the end of that page, Constance had written, *And that, dear girl, is the brief story of my life. But what of yours?*

A girl is in a room, alone. Reading by a single lantern, the next page began.

The girl hears something. The ceiling above her head creaked, and Clara looked up.

The girl looks up.

Clara finished the action before she read the words. She tried to convince herself that the noise had been in her head, and that the words in front of her were just a coincidence.

There are ten footsteps, then ten more. A strange man is in the house.

Clara's mother wasn't supposed to be home for hours. The lights were out upstairs. Clara listened, and stared at the ceiling as if willing it to be silent.

She heard nothing.

She realized she'd been holding her breath and she exhaled, then took in a deep breath.

That's when she heard the footsteps. She covered her mouth to stop the scream that was rising in her throat. She counted the first ten steps, heavy on the floor above her head. After that, she stopped counting. She didn't care how many there were.

Someone was in the house, just as it said in the book!

She looked around. There was no landline down here, and her cell phone was upstairs, charging. The basement room didn't have a door with a lock, so if anyone came down the stairs, she'd be trapped.

Then she heard the front door slam shut.

He left, she told herself. Whoever it was who had been in the house had left. It finally occurred to her to look back down at the book, to see what happened next.

The girl is done reading. There was no more writing on the page. Clara shut the book. There was no sense tempting fate.

She waited a long time before walking carefully up the basement stairs, and when she did, she clutched the Victorian snow globe tightly in one hand. If needed, she could throw the snow globe, which was heavy and hard, at an intruder.

She stepped carefully on each stair, trying to be as quiet as possible. Once she reached the top, she swung the door open quickly—no sense losing the element of surprise—but the kitchen was dark. Rather than turn on the light, she listened.

Apart from a slow drip in the sink, she heard nothing. Clara waited for her eyes to adjust to the dark. The kitchen was empty. She peered out the window, checking the porch and the front yard. The street was silent and still. In the moonlight she could see the hulking mass of the boulder, with Biskopskulla Bed and Breakfast etched into its side.

Satisfied that whoever had been in the house—what a horrifying thought!—had now left, Clara locked the front door.

With her heart still racing, Clara thought a glass of orange juice and a peanut butter-and-jelly half-sandwich might help calm her down.

She was halfway through the living room when she saw the intruder.

A big man, wearing a hat and jacket, sat in the armchair next to the window. Half in darkness, and half illuminated by moonlight, Clara could see a shotgun with what looked like a thirty-inch barrel lying across his lap.

Clara screamed and threw her sandwich, which bounced harmlessly off his chest.

7

I am so sorry," Clara said to the man twenty minutes later. "We had no idea that Grandma took reservations for the bed and breakfast so far in advance. We would have called you and canceled if we'd known."

"No, no, don't apologize," said the man, who had introduced himself as Al. "I'm sorry about your grandmother. And I should've called ahead. It's just this hunting trip kinda snuck up on me. It's been a busy fall and I almost forgot about the reservation myself until night before last."

When Al had arrived and found no one home, he'd sat down on an easy chair in the living room to wait, he told her, and fallen asleep.

"I am so sorry I frightened you," he said, "and I am sure I can find a motel for tonight."

"No worries," said Clara. "Yes, there's a hotel near the freeway, I think."

"One word of advice," Al said, on his way out the door. "You might want to get rid of that boulder that says *bed and breakfast*. I sure as heck wouldn't've just walked in if I hadn't seen that. Just my two cents."

"Thanks, mister," Clara said. She was still a little shaken, but thoroughly relieved that Al wasn't here to kill her.

"All right, you have a good night, and be sure to lock up now, hear?"

"For sure," Clara said. She intended to stay awake to tell her mother what had happened, but she fell asleep on the couch with all the lights on.

When Clara's mom heard about the intruder, she was livid. "First, when I'm not home, you lock the door!" she demanded. "And second, we're going to have to do something about that big rock."

Clara's mom looked up landscaping companies online, but when she described the boulder over the phone to them, the prices they quoted for its removal started at five hundred dollars.

"Why don't I find a tarp to cover it up with?" Clara asked.

"Mmm. Good idea but I don't know that that would look so nice," Clara's mom said. "I'll ask around."

Two mornings later, Clara's mom had a solution. A friend from work, called Sylvia, had suggested contacting her nephew, who worked at the cemetery and handled heavy stuff all the time. Sylvia's nephew was coming by later that day to take a look at their boulder.

"Sounds like a plan," Clara said. When she arrived home from school that afternoon, a large green pickup truck was parked outside their house. Three men were climbing out as she approached. Her mom came out of the house to greet them.

"Hey, Ms. Hutchins," one of the men said. "Sylvia said you need some help getting this rock out. Don't worry, we'll have it taken care of in no time."

Clara sat on the front porch steps to watch the activity. The three men used shovels to dig around the edges of the boulder, and then they set up a large three-legged metal tripod over the stone. They tied nylon straps around the sides of the boulder to secure it and fastened these to a chain hooked to a winch in the truck. Once the boulder was out of the ground, they swung it toward the back of the truck, and then two of them pushed it further onto the truck bed while the other gradually released the chain. The whole process took less than thirty minutes. The men even emptied a metal drum full of earth into the hole and tamped it down so the hole left by the boulder was neatly filled.

"Now *that* was impressive," Clara's mom said with a smile, as she carried a twelve-pack of beer down the porch stairs to the men in the truck. Clara raised an eyebrow, and her mother laughed. "I'm just doing what I was told, Clara. Beer for boulders."

When the truck was fully loaded, two men put away the tripod while Sylvia's nephew came up to the porch.

"My dad was actually the one who engraved the words *Bed and Breakfast* on that stone," he told them. "That must have been, shoot, twenty years ago. The next time you see her, she'll probably have someone's name on her. Here lies so-and-so," he said. Clara thought it was funny to refer to rocks as female.

"Thank you so much!" Clara's mom said as she handed him the beer.

"Oh, well, isn't that nice of you!" he said. "Listen, I'm really sorry about your mom," he added. "She was a real nice lady. If you ever feel like visiting her, feel free to stop by and say hi."

Of course, Clara thought. *There's only one cemetery around here. This guy works where Grandma's buried.*

8

For the next few days, Clara was afraid to read any more of the book in the basement. Now that she'd sold all the antique dolls online, Clara decided it was time to move the curio cabinet out of her bedroom for good.

She felt a little guilty. Maybe those dolls *were* special to Grandma. She'd never know. She tried to remember what her grandmother was like, and felt sad that it was difficult for her.

Sliding the cabinet away from the wall, she discovered a shoebox, covered in dust, that had been tucked underneath. Within it she found assorted newspaper clippings about her mother's college volleyball games and an envelope marked *Clara*, with a heart drawn around her name. Inside the envelope, she found a handful of baby pictures, some school photos of her from over the years, and a curious wooden pendant of a delicate butterfly, its wings detailed in gold wire. Clara had never seen anything like it before. Perhaps it is a family heirloom, she mused, one that her grandmother meant her to have. It was nice to imagine that just as she had been thinking about Grandma Catherine, maybe, sometime in the past, Grandma had sat in this room thinking about her.

She slipped the necklace around her neck, feeling comforted. Maybe this old house wasn't as scary as it seemed. That night she read two more pages in Constance Love's book, and although what she read was confusing, it disturbed her so much that she put it down after two pages and decided that she was never going to read the book alone again. Ever. It was just too unsettling. She wanted to share the book with someone who would understand, and she thought she knew just who that someone might be.

The next morning was the Hawley Douglas Crazy Bomber 5k, and Clara was determined to find an opportunity after the race to speak to Gary. She had no idea as she ate her breakfast that by the end of the day, she would be witness to a crime.

One of the most curious Biskopskulla traditions was the annual opening of Erik Mattsson's tomb. While most of the historic places in the village were open to tourists all spring, summer, and fall, the tomb of Erik Mattsson was opened to the public for only one hour per year, according to the instructions of the villagers who had laid him to rest in 1849. Rumor had it they wanted to make sure that someone would always check to see if he'd risen from the dead.

It was a gloomy day. Clara wore black sweatpants and a light jacket over her sweatshirt. The morning air was still chilly, and she folded her arms around herself and tucked her hands into her armpits as she stepped out of the car.

"You okay?" her mother asked.

"Yeah. Fine," Clara said. "You sure you don't want to run, Mom? It'll be fun."

"Not a chance. I will wait at the finish line and drink cocoa while you suffer. That is my role today."

The town square consisted of a few businesses surrounding a park that was really just a patch of grass with a concrete marker. On the marker was a plaque proclaiming that in 1984 the United States Department of the Interior had declared the Biskopskulla Colony Historic District to be a National Historic Landmark. Today, the marker was draped in colorful crepe paper. Clara registered with a lady at a folding table and was given a bib with the number 28 on it. She found Gary talking to his mother. Gary was wearing a T-shirt and shorts.

"Aren't you cold?" Clara asked, jumping up and down for warmth.

"Oh, you are in for a *heck* of a winter if you think this is cold, A Clara."

"Hi, Clara," Mrs. Mahler said, with a smile. "I am so glad you are joining us. Gary and I are both trying to beat our best times, so we might not keep pace with you. But we will look forward to seeing you at the finishing line."

"That's okay. I wasn't going to try to win or anything," Clara confided. "I am just going to try to finish."

Gary scowled. "Way to take all the fun out of beating you."

Clara noticed a few of her teachers among the runners. Mr. Hawthorne and his wife wore matching track pants. Mr. Froehlich was stretching his calf muscles, and Mrs. Maynard was chatting with another lady as she poured water into lots of little white cups.

Myron and Kaitlyn pushed their way through the crowds. "Hi, Clara. Hi, Gary," Kaitlyn exclaimed. "What a *mellifluous* morning it is!"

"Are you guys running too?" Clara asked hopefully.

"No," Myron said. "I'm just here to help my mom with the bake sale."

"I've just come to watch," Kaitlyn said. "But isn't it funny how we combine exercise with sweets?"

"It's the American way, Kaitlyn-with-a-K," Gary said with a shrug.

"It's not the most *efficacious* way to celebrate town history," Kaitlyn said, and Gary rolled his eyes.

"Watch your mouth, K! There are *ladies* present."

The runners gathered near the Honey Drop Pub, a long and narrow building of gray brick. Two picnic tables, covered with plastic tablecloths, were piled high with cookies, muffins, and quick breads: pumpkin, banana, and—especially—zucchini. Zucchini bread, zucchini muffins, zucchini brownies…Clara thought of zucchini as a vegetable and was astonished that it was an ingredient in so many baked goods.

The sidewalk in front of the pub was lined with red bricks, each stamped with the words *Biskopskulla Heritage Association* along with a person's name. Clara figured the naming rights to each brick had been sold over the years as a way to raise funds for the association.

A portable podium was stationed between the two tables, with a red, white, and blue battery-powered megaphone resting on top. Alice Dewar, the town's mayor, approached the podium to a smattering of high-speed applause from Myron, who clearly felt a keen responsibility to be an enthusiastic audience member.

"One hundred years ago—" Alice began.

"Actually, a hundred and one," Mrs. Mahler muttered under her breath.

"Just after midnight," the mayor continued, "Hawley Charles Douglas placed four sticks of dynamite into the foundations of the only two saloons in Biskopskulla. Then he tried to blow up the village church, perhaps because he'd heard the pastor kept a cask of wine in the public room. We know he used ten sticks of dynamite that night, but the rest of his stockpiles of explosives have never been found, so— who knows? One day his ghost may come back and finish the deed." A half-hearted laugh rippled through the crowd.

Gary groaned. "She makes that joke every year."

Mrs. Mahler sighed. "The last *three* mayors made that joke every year."

"Today," the mayor continued, "we turn these tragic events into a celebration, beginning here at the first saloon to be bombed, the Honey Drop Pub. The owners, Sally and Mike Winthrop, have been kind enough to donate bottled water for all of our runners today."

She stopped to lead the audience in a brief bout of clapping.

"The second pub to be bombed was sadly torn down in the 1970s, so we will end our race at the still-standing and restored Biskopskulla Colony Church. Thanks to Boy Scout Troop 359 for volunteering with the cleanup"—another smattering of applause—"and, because today is September 22, the tomb of Erik Mattsson will be opened to the public between noon and one p.m. today. Please, respect the church rules and do not take photographs inside the tomb. There are some historic artifacts inside, as well as the sarcophagus of Erik Mattsson, the town's founder. Remember, if you miss this chance to see inside, you'll have to wait a whole year before you can see it again."

The runners lined up, wearing their numbered bibs. Some of the students got down in a crouch, their hands on the ground, as if competing in the Olympics. "It's not a sprint," Gary muttered, rolling his eyes.

A man standing next to the mayor raised a starting gun into the air. "Runners, get ready!" he yelled. "Go!"

When the gun went off, Clara ran, reducing her pace after a minute or two. Gary and his mother pulled ahead as Clara settled into a slow but steady clip. The crowd of runners began to thin out quite quickly, until Clara was running by herself, with a pack of faster runners barely visible ahead and a scattering of slower runners behind. The brick sidewalk gave way to a plain dirt path, which then wound its way between a grove of trees. A large sheet of posterboard, decorated with red, yellow, and blue balloons, had been taped to the tree, the number 2 written in purple magic marker. The two-kilometer distance marker. Three to go, Clara thought, gasping to catch her breath.

Clara ran past the village's small business district, which included one of the town's two restaurants, and then veered right, down a paved road, and through the gates of the colony's historic cemetery.

At least they don't have us running over graves, she thought as she turned onto the road that ran through the cemetery. Newer graves had fresh flowers on them, but others, toward the back fence line, appeared much older with headstones that were crumbled and weatherworn. Clara wondered if Constance Love had been buried in the cemetery, and whether she could visit her grave sometime. At the end of the cemetery was a poster with the number 4.

Oh, thank goodness! she thought. *I'm almost done.* Thinking about it made her feet hurt.

Eventually she could see the finish line ahead of her, as she ran through an empty field toward the back of the old church. The runners in front of her crossed the finish line, then walked out of view around the side of the church toward the front where the tables had been set up.

Clara focused on the church, striving for a final burst of speed. A slight movement in the church steeple drew her attention. The steeple rose from the center of the church's angled roof. But where the rest of the church windows were glass, the steeple had open-air windows that resembled horizontal blinds of painted wood.

The sun was rising behind the church, and Clara could see the outline of the church bell clearly. She could see something moving between the slats, within the steeple. At first she thought it might be a bird or an animal, but then she saw that it was a person. Curious, she stopped to watch as she caught her breath. The figure appeared to be doing something to the top of the bell, then, a moment later, they were gone.

Probably someone making sure the bell is working, she thought. After all, they would probably be ringing it sometime today.

Clara ran across a white chalk finish line as a man in a white shirt yelled, "Twenty-eight twenty! Congratulations! Drink some water!" A table had been set up between the church entrance and Erik Mattsson's tomb, with plastic cups, bottles of water, and pitchers of juice and Gatorade. Clara poured herself a glass of orange juice, then looked around for her mother and the Mahlers.

She found them all together—Gary looking distinctly uncomfortable as their mothers bonded over Styrofoam cups of coffee. Behind them, near the back corner of the church, a young man was setting up a velvet rope at the doorway to a small stone mausoleum, even though only two people stood in line. Erik Mattsson's tomb, apparently, didn't draw much of a crowd.

"A Clara!" Gary yelled with relief as she approached. "What time did you get?"

"I got twenty-eight minutes and twenty seconds, but I probably could have shaved off at least five seconds if only there had been someone cheering me on at the finish line," she said, pretend-glaring at her mother.

"Sorry, kiddo," her mom said with a laugh, "you were too fast. I thought I had at least a half an hour to get into position."

"False alarm!" a man shouted nearby, his voice hoarse. They all turned to see a stocky man in layers of sweatshirts, his dirty sweatpants cinched with a black dress belt, lying on the pavement.

"False alarm!" he cried again, as he scrambled awkwardly to his feet.

"Are you all right?" Clara's mom asked.

"Yep, yep. False alarm. Not my t-t-time yet." He smiled sweetly at Clara's mother. "But ain't you just a s-s-sandwich?" he added, before walking away.

"That's Raymond," Mrs. Mahler said. "Raymond Bergstrom. He's…" She paused a moment, searching for the right words. "He's working through some issues these days."

"I can see that," Clara's mom said.

Suddenly, a loud CRASH drew everyone's attention. They heard a terrible splintering of wood coming from the other side of the church, followed by the sounds of shattering glass and crunching metal.

Confusion reigned as everyone raced around the side of the church to see what was happening. Rounding the corner, Clara saw a big yellow-and-black school bus, its windshield smashed and the front part of its roof dented in. Gary came to a breathless halt by her side. "What happened?" he gasped.

The roof of the church was a mess. The steeple had a gaping hole in its side and a wedge of ancient shingles had been gouged out of the angled roof. Resting on top of the nose of the bus was what looked like a corroded metal acorn.

It was the church bell.

"Who's in charge of the church?" she asked Gary.

"There's a curator, but I don't see him right now. He sometimes works with Mom when she does the ghost tours."

Clara decided she should tell the mayor, who was busy talking to a young police deputy who had arrived on the scene.

"What's the matter?" the mayor asked Clara, impatiently.

"I just wanted to let you know that someone was working on the bell in the church steeple before, when I was finishing the race. I just wanted to make sure that person was okay."

"Nobody's in the church today," the mayor told her. "It's been locked all day and won't be open to the public again until the renovations are complete. And the construction workers only work weekdays." She then turned her attention back to the deputy, who was ordering everyone back from the bus.

Just then a man Clara didn't recognize pushed through the milling crowd and made his way to the deputy. After whispering urgently in his ear, the deputy spoke urgently to the mayor, then all three walked briskly around to the other side of the church.

"Let's go see what's going on," Gary said as they watched the three adults walk off. Together they ran around the opposite side of the church, coming to a sudden halt before the tomb of Erik Mattson. The three adults, as well as a number of police officers, had disappeared into the tomb.

When Clara and Gary tried to follow them, an officer came out to stop them.

"You can't come in here, kids. This is a crime scene."

"But the tomb is supposed to be open to the public today, right?" Gary asked loudly, motioning for Clara to get a peek inside while he distracted the officer. "I've been waiting months and months, and I just want—"

Peering around the officer, Clara could see faded inscriptions on the tomb walls and a waist-high granite sarcophagus in the center. A stone slab—the lid of the sarcophagus—had been slid aside and the lid of a wooden coffin inside had been wrenched open.

Within the coffin, Clara could see a strange-looking pair of shoes, and then she realized—those shoes were on the feet of a corpse! And that corpse was Erik Mattsson!

One of the men—who Clara would later learn was the village's curator—reached inside the sarcophagus and pulled out an object that looked like a knife.

"Kids, you're going to have to leave—" the officer said impatiently.

Then, however, the deputy came out of the tomb, his gaze landing on Clara.

"Young lady," he called to her. "Did I hear you say you saw somebody inside the church?"

Clara, distracted, took a moment to answer. She'd been thinking about Constance Love's book, and something truly strange that she'd read the previous night.

9

The next day, Clara decided to share the book with Gary.

She felt she could trust him to keep the secret, but it also seemed that Constance Love wanted her to tell him.

She'd invited him over to work on their art projects together and thought they could do that in the basement—the perfect opportunity to share the book with him. This book is more than a historic artifact, she thought, thrilled but scared at the same time.

This might actually be *real magic*.

When Gary arrived, they carried boxes of art supplies and poster board down to the basement, which had become a hangout room for Clara. "At least it's not one of those creepy dark basements," Gary said approvingly. "This is pretty cool."

Clara had to agree. The décor of the house hadn't been updated since the 70s, so everything from the attic that wasn't an antique still had a cool retro look to it. The basement's cement floor had been covered by a green shag rug, and the walls had been painted a pretty terracotta. Clara had hung brightly colored posters on the walls, and two old but comfy easy chairs provided seating. The single hanging light bulb had been inserted into a colorful cloth lampshade.

"Did you hear anything else about the grave robbing?" Gary asked, excited by the prospect of a real unsolved crime happening in their small town.

"Not really," Clara said, "They think there was someone inside the church who wasn't supposed to be there."

"Yeah, but do they think both things are related? I mean, obviously they are. Someone rigged the church bell to fall and create a distraction, and then they robbed Erik Mattsson's grave when no one was looking."

"But why? What did they take? As far as anyone could tell, nothing was missing."

"You said the coffin was wrenched open? Which means that whatever it was the perp was after, it was buried with Mattsson," Gary said. "That is so cool."

"There's something else I want to show you," Clara said, retrieving the book from its hiding place in a basket under a stack of cushions.

Gary was quiet as she told him about how she had found the book, how she had figured out how to open the box, and about the pages she had read so far.

She showed him the parts about the lantern and the strange man in the house and described her frightening encounter with the hunter upstairs. Then she turned to the page most recently uncovered. This was what she had been dying to show him.

In flowery script, in the center of the page, were these words:

There Shall come a time of Great Awakening
A Danger for all Biskopskulla
A Baneful and Cursed One shall Return
He shall have a Black Eye and a Horn for a Hand
When the Bell falls on the Bee
And the Day and Night are equal
Be wary, dear girl
The Storm of Blood awaits.

Gary looked up from the book, a strange expression on his face. "This is heavy. Your great-great-great-grandmother wrote a book of predictions just for you. And it sounds like she's…warning you."

Clara's heart sank. She'd secretly hoped that Gary would dismiss the book as nonsense, that he'd tell her the whole idea of Constance Love communicating from the past was ridiculous. Then she'd have an excuse not to worry. "Well," she said. "I'm not one hundred percent sure it's really meant for me. I mean, I just happened to find it. And I am sure there are lots of girls around called Clara, right?" she asked hopefully.

"Not in this town," Gary said darkly. "You've figured out the part about the bell and the bee, haven't you?"

"Well, a school bus looks an awful lot like a bee, with its black and yellow stripes, don't you think?"

"Yeah, but then that means the time of great awakening has come," Gary said, "and a baneful and cursed one has returned."

"I think the bell has to fall on the bee *and* the day and night have to be equal before that happens."

"Clara, are you kidding? That part is obvious. The Hawley Douglas race is always scheduled on the autumnal equinox. That's why it was on September 22 this year."

"I'm not into calendar trivia, Gary."

"Fine. The autumnal equinox is the day in the fall when the time between sunrise and sunset is almost exactly twelve hours—half the day. On an equinox, the day and night are equal."

"That makes it…scarier. I mean, I kind of was hoping you were going to tell me this was all some silly coincidence. Now I'm a little freaked out."

"Me too," Gary admitted. "Who else have you told about this?"

"No one yet. I don't think I'm supposed to." Clara turned the page and showed him the writing on the opposite side.

Dear girl, if you tell the boy, tell no one else.

Gary whistled. "Okay, first of all, what the heck? It sounds like you could have told other people, if you *hadn't* told me. Second of all, 'the boy?' I have a name."

"I don't think you should get bent out of shape about that. And, I don't know, I guess I thought she was saying I *should* tell the boy? Like, I was already thinking about it, and then I saw that, and it felt like she was giving me permission."

"You were thinking about me?"

"I was thinking about telling you about the horrifying book of predictions I found in my basement. Yes."

"Well, okay then."

He picked the book up and turned it around in his hands. "We have to read the rest of it. I think we need to figure out how this ends. And what is up with this baneful, cursed dude."

Clara showed him the page with the warning *Books are read from front to back*. But he was not dissuaded.

"Just one page," he said. "Let's do the second-to-last page, just in case."

"Just in case of what?"

"In case the last page brings about the end of the world or something."

10

No luck. Gary and Clara discovered that whenever they carefully opened the book to a later page, it would invariably be blank.

They tried this four times and even picked a page just a few pages further than Clara had already read. *This* page did indeed have text on it.

It said: *Dear girl, is your curiosity satisfied?*

Clara shivered.

"Do you believe it?" Gary asked. It took Clara a moment to realize his question wasn't rhetorical.

"I think I do," she said.

"I think I do too."

They could hear Clara's mom coming down the stairs. Clara quickly set a piece of poster board over the old book.

"How is it going, kids?" Clara's mom asked.

"Still figuring out what to draw," Clara replied, gesturing at the empty poster board.

"Well, I brought you some cookies. Maybe that will help with inspiration."

"Thanks, Ms. H.," Gary said brightly. "Did you make these yourself?"

Clara stifled a laugh.

"I opened the package myself," Clara's mom said with a smile, "which is almost like making them myself. Anyway, I'll let you two get back to it. Will you be staying for dinner, Gary?"

"Thanks, Ms. H., but I have to get home for dinner tonight," Gary said.

"Well, some other time," Clara's mom said on her way out the door.

Clara and Gary waited in silence for a minute, until they

could hear the upstairs door shut. "I think we should unseal all of the pages first, then read the rest of it at all at once," Gary said.

"Why?" Clara asked.

"What if there's a problem? What if something gets ripped? What if there's a page with illegible writing? Or what if we read something horrible?"

"Okay," Clara said. "But we have to read it in order, no reading ahead. The book is pretty clear about that."

"Right, no reading ahead," Gary agreed.

The two of them spent the rest of the afternoon meticulously getting the pages unstuck from one another, careful not to look at what was written on the yellowed paper. When it was time for Gary to leave, they were nearly finished.

"When do you want to meet again?" Clara asked him.

"We'd better make it soon. After all," he said, "a Baneful and Cursed One is on his way."

11

Clara finished her watercolor painting of the bed and breakfast, her first project in art class. She was quite pleased with the result and thought she'd captured the late-afternoon shadows on the brick walls, and the few leaves left on the trees. The photo must have been taken in autumn, she thought. The house had hardly changed at all over the years. Clara signed her name with a flourish just underneath the boulder, which she had painted in with a light gray.

For her next project Clara decided to make an ink drawing of Constance Love. Although no known photographs existed of Constance, Clara decided she would use a drawing from the old history book as an inspiration. Then she had the idea of copying a photo of her great-grandmother instead—she'd been Constance's granddaughter, after all. Surely there was a family resemblance?

As Clara erased the line of Constance's jaw for the tenth time, Gary said, "My uncle is visiting this week, but he leaves on Friday. Are you free on Saturday?"

"Don't we have a scholastic bowl competition that day?" Clara asked.

"Nope, that's next Saturday."

"All right, I'll tell my mom we need to study for a test."

"Well, we do have math tests next week."

On Saturday, Gary came over. He brought a plastic container of spring rolls that his mom had made for Clara and her mother. They retreated to the basement, and they spent the next two hours going through the book, page by page, deciphering the predictions of Constance Love. Gary took notes in a three-subject notebook and occasionally he took photos with his phone.

The reading was dull at times, and at others, incredibly exciting. The book included a lot of lists and recipes, and Clara didn't know if she was the intended audience for a buttermilk biscuit recipe or if there were only so many places to write stuff down in the Love household in the 1860s.

One page was particularly cryptic. *I see the Cursed one; he shall bring about the Storm of Death. Afterward I have no Sight.*

"I wish she could be more specific," Clara said. "If she could really see the future, why does she have to write every sentence like it's some vague fortune cookie?"

"I know, right?" Gary agreed. "And here it says Storm of Death, but a few pages ago it was Storm of Blood. So which is it, Death or Blood?" Gary asked. "And what does that even mean?"

"I don't know, but either way it can't be good. In fact, it sounds awful. Just awful."

"What it sounds like to me," said Gary, "is that this is the last thing she can predict. Storm of Death. Then, done."

"Like her magic powers were reaching their limit?"

"Or maybe she can't see anything beyond that because there's nothing left to be seen."

Clara bit her lip. "We have to keep reading." She sighed. "I wonder how it all worked."

"How what worked?"

"Her predictions. Did they come to her in a dream, or did she have visions she couldn't control, or did she choose a time and place in the future and then see that?"

"Or something else," Gary said.

"Or something else."

"And...what about all the other stuff that has happened since she died?" Gary said. "I mean, two world wars, the Spanish flu, space travel...was that just not important enough to write about? Why is she only seeing our present time?"

"I just wish she'd be clearer about whatever it is she wants us to know," Clara said with a sigh.

Gary turned the page.

At the top, in the same distinct script, was one word: *Ask*.

The two of them looked at each other wordlessly. Clara's eyes grew wide. Gary took Clara's hands and placed them together on the open page of the book. "What is your name?" he said loudly and slowly.

Gary turned the page.

There were three words now: *Ask in writing*.

"Do you think we should write in it?" Gary asked, taking a pen out of his pocket.

"It's my book," Clara said. "I'll write." In small block letters, she wrote *What is your name?* Then she turned the page.

The writing looked ancient, the flowery script faded on the page, weathered by the ravages of time. And yet—it was a response to the question Clara had just asked.

You know my name, dear girl. I am Constance Love.

Gary whistled, nervous. It was like a stage magician's trick, Clara thought, where a message had been sealed in an envelope that a member of the audience had been sitting on for the entire show. But there was no way this could be a trick, she thought. She had decided what question to ask just seconds ago. But somehow, in the nineteenth century, Constance Love knew what she was going to write today.

How do you know, Clara wrote, *things that haven't happened yet?* She turned the page.

I can see the tomorrows of certain things, of certain places, and of certain people when I touch them. I saw you opening this book, dear girl, and I knew I should write for you.

Gary frowned. "This is so...Man, this is weird." He thought a moment. "That would explain why she didn't notice major world events. I mean, if her abilities to see the future were limited to stuff she could touch. Um, can I write something?" Clara wordlessly handed him the pen.

Do you see us now? He turned the page.

I see a girl and a boy. I see my book—old and mildewed. With great difficulty, I can read what is written.

Clara took the pen back.

Are we in danger? she wrote.

Dear girl, and boy, you are in grave, grave danger. You will soon meet a man who is not a man. He will set in motion a cataclysm when the shortest day turns into the longest night. Untold numbers will die.

"That probably means the winter solstice," Gary said. "It's the longest night of the year."

"I know that," Clara said. "But I'm a little more concerned about the 'grave danger' part." She *did* know about solstices—she'd read about them in the library the day before. The winter solstice was the shortest day of the year, and the summer solstice was the longest. "The winter solstice will be on December 21 this year," she said.

"That doesn't give us much time," Gary said.

"Whoever this Cursed One is," Clara said, "and whatever he's planning to do…we have something he doesn't."

"What?" Gary asked,

"Constance Love," she replied, picking up the pen again.

Clara wrote a numbered list of questions on the page.

1. Who is he?

2. If he is not a man, what is he?

3. Why is he going to harm us?

4. What is he going to do?

5. How can we protect ourselves?

Gary placed his index finger behind the corner of the page. "Here goes nothing," he said, flipping to the next page.

He goes by many names. He is a witch, and he is old, older than the trees in the village. His survival depends on the death of others. The enchantment necessary to further his life demands a cataclysm. I believe there is no earthly way to stop him, save a stronger enchantment—a Spell of Protection. Perhaps a girl of my blood could enact such a spell.

And you, dear girl, have my blood.

Gary cracked his knuckles. "She knows. She knows that you're her granddaughter—her great, great, whatever granddaughter."

"Can we focus on the part about my blood? Maybe the part about the death of others?"

"Hey," Gary protested. "She said I was in danger too. Don't turn the page yet. We have to take stock."

"Okay—"

"First off," Gary said. "We know it's real. I mean, if we showed this to someone, they wouldn't believe that we were writing questions to answers that were written a hundred and forty years ago. But we both saw this, right here. We know it's not a hoax. Next point: if there really is someone who is going to harm us, how are we going to protect ourselves? I mean, if it's a witch, a real witch, what can we do? Call the police?"

"They'd never believe us," Clara agreed.

"What we need is a witch. Our own witch," he said.

"I think maybe Constance wrote this book to help us," she said.

"And I think we need that help," Gary said.

Clara put the pen to the page. *Constance*, she began writing. *Please tell us: what should we do?* She swallowed hard, then turned the page to see her response.

At first, she thought the next page was covered in dense, indecipherable scribbles.

But looking closer, she could see that the page was covered in a tiny, cursive script. Constance had written her an answer—it was ten pages long, and reading it took Gary and Clara the rest of the day, with Gary taking detailed notes in his notebook.

Constance revealed that she had spent the better part of a year considering the answer to that one question. She devoted the rest of the book to solving their problem, and providing an explanation of the objects they needed to find. But she didn't tell them *where* to look. They finished the book in silence, as the gravity of the task ahead weighed upon them.

They had reached the end of the book. The rest was up to them.

After Gary left, Clara wondered if she should tell her mother. The book seemed to warn against telling people about it, but Clara wasn't accustomed to keeping secrets from her own mother.

Here's the deal, Mom, Clara imagined herself saying, *I just found out that someone is coming to Biskopskulla to cause some kind of massacre.*

Constance Love wrote to me from over a hundred years ago that he'll have a black eye and a horn for his hand.

There was no way Mom would believe any of this, Clara concluded. It was up to her and Gary.

Clara copied their to-do list onto the back of a postcard she'd found in her dresser featuring a picture of a local museum.

1. Find the bones of Constance Love

2. Find the spell book

3. Find an artifact that "detects enchantments?"

4. Avoid detection by the "Baneful & Cursed One"

5. ...Stop the Storm of Death/Blood

The "spell book" was referenced in the last few pages of Constance's book—that is, the last few pages of Constance's *first* book. She wrote that it was too dangerous to describe the Spell of Protection in a single volume, so she promised to write more about the spell in a second book, one which Clara would need to find.

She also mentioned a special, magical artifact, something that could detect "the presence of an enchantment." Constance seemed to think it would help them in the event that someone cursed them.

Constance had also been very clear that they would need to find her actual remains for the magic to work, even though she provided no clear information about where her body might be found.

About that corpse, Clara wondered. *Where on earth could it be?*

12

The morning that Clara and Gary planned to visit the village cemetery was, so far, the coldest morning of the year. This was fitting, Clara thought, because cemeteries had always given her a chill.

She met Gary near the colony church.

"A Clara!" Gary called out as she approached. They walked to the cemetery without talking much, Gary kicking loose rocks ahead on the asphalt road.

"Do you know anyone who's buried here?" Clara asked, gesturing toward the cemetery.

"Yeah, I mean…my brother," Gary said.

"That's right," Clara said. She didn't apologize, because Gary didn't seem to like that sort of thing. Instead, she changed the subject. "How old are the oldest graves here?"

"Oh, man, 1840s at least. The colony was founded in 1846. There were about fifteen hundred people and by the time they finally got here it was almost winter. So they started losing people right off the bat. It was really cold, and they lived in dugouts."

"It must have been awful," Clara said.

"I tend to think everything was awful before the twentieth century. I would have just walked around all day wishing I could brush my teeth."

"So there are graves here that are 160 years old. Cool."

"Yeah. When I was in grade school, we had a field trip to the cemetery where we did crayon rubbings of some of the older graves. A few of them have little engravings, but most of them are pretty plain. Around the 1880s they started in-cluding creepier stuff, little angels and skulls on the graves," Gary said.

"Does your mom give tours of the cemetery?" Clara asked.

"Of course she does," said Gary. "What kind of ghost tour skips the scariest part?"

They had arrived at the westernmost corner of the Biskopskulla Village Cemetery. It was a grim place, Clara realized, but it didn't look particularly special. There was no fence around the cemetery, except along the far side, where a wall separated the graveyard from a cornfield. An unpaved road, little more than two-wheel ruts with grass in between, led through the center of the cemetery.

The newer gravestones lay to the right, the older stones to the left. At the far end of the cemetery, an excavator, a piece of earth-moving equipment, sat motionless. It was about thirteen feet tall, with a hydraulic arm reaching thirty feet into the air.

"I want to find my grandmother's grave," Clara said. "Then we can look at the older stuff. Maybe we'll see something."

"You know we're not going to find Constance Love's grave, right? There is no record of where she was buried."

"You think that's a coincidence?" Clara asked.

"No, I think it was absolutely intentional. They wanted to bury the witch and keep her hidden. It's like that saying, lock her up and throw away the key," Gary said.

Clara found her grandmother's grave without much difficulty. *Catherine Anderson Hutchins. 1928-2010.* It seemed so long ago, 1928. Clara thought of what she knew about the 1920s. Henry Ford was selling Model T cars, and every single one was black. The Great Depression hadn't even started yet. World War II was years away. What must it have been like for Catherine Anderson Hutchins to live through so much? Next to Catherine's grave was that of her husband, Herman Hutchins. Clara had never known him, nor had her mother. He'd died in 1972, when Clara's mother was just a baby.

In the oldest part of the cemetery Clara saw a wooden post with a crosspiece from which a large wooden sign hung. It read *Biskopskulla Colony Cemetery. Established 1846* and underneath that, in small letters, it said, *Illinois State Historical Society, 1987.*

The headstones here were very plain, and the inscriptions tended to feature just a few last names: Anderson. Barlow. Ericson. Erickson. Johnson. Those buried here often shared the same first names, as well: Andrew Anderson. Andrew G. Anderson. Andrew Howard Anderson. Et cetera.

"Look," Gary said, pointing at a stone slab, smaller than the others, inscribed with the word *Baby* and the date *1851.* "He didn't live long enough even to get a name," he said.

"Or she," Clara said, quietly. The two of them looked at the simple stone in silence.

Without warning, the excavator behind them roared to life, the sudden rumble of the diesel engine so loud that Clara, startled, fell backward.

"Golly," she said, rising to her feet.

"You've got to do something about that foul mouth," Gary joked.

The two of them watched as the excavator carved a hole in the earth at the edge of the cemetery.

"Wouldn't it be *cool* if he turned up, like, a hand?" Gary said.

"Ugh, no," Clara said. "It would not be cool at all."

The two of them took a few steps away from the excavator—it was *so* loud—and its driver seemed to notice them for the first time. He appeared startled to see them. He turned off the machine, climbed down from the cab, and walked toward them.

He was tall, well over six feet, with a large forehead, and short black hair that stuck out on one side as if he'd slept on it wrong. He wore dirty carpenter pants, and an olive-green shirt with an absurd number of pockets, and a work glove on his right hand; the left glove was stuffed in his shirt pocket.

As he glanced at Clara, she realized that each of his eyes was a different color. His right eye was very dark and his left eye was a pale blue. Clara stared at them, and then realized that she was staring, so she dropped her gaze to the ground.

"You children should not be here," the tall man said, his voice faintly accented.

"What's your name, sir? I'm Gary," Gary said, with mock politeness.

"I'm Tad," the man replied. "Tad Trumpeter."

The name didn't suit him at all, Clara thought. *Tad* suggested a scrappy child, not this tall man with messy hair.

"Why are you digging there?" Gary asked. "I have some family buried in this cemetery—we both do," he added, as if this gave him license to inquire.

"The village council hired me. The rain has been washing off the topsoil. Not good in a cemetery, is that? But we'll get a drainage ditch along either side here, and line them with rock, and everyone's loved ones can sleep safe and sound."

"What if you dig up a person?" Gary asked.

"There's no one buried in the ground along this edge," Tad said. Then, suddenly, he froze, so still that it seemed he wasn't breathing. His eyes darted toward Clara, then back to Gary. "Unless…you know something?"

Clara shivered in spite of herself. An uncomfortable silence followed as Tad scrutinized them through narrowed eyes. "No, of course you don't," he said. "I've got to get back to work, so best if you two ran along. This work will be done in a day or two, and you can come back and visit then."

Gary looked as if he was going to protest, so Clara piped up. "Sure, thanks for all the work you're doing, keeping our loved ones safe and all." She grabbed Gary by the elbow and together they made their way back toward the entrance of the cemetery.

Tad returned to the excavator, and Clara saw the name

stenciled along the side: *T. Trumpeter Excavation & Demolition.*

Gary couldn't help being a smart aleck. "Goodbye, Mr. Trumpeter! It was nice meeting you!" he shouted brightly as they walked away.

Tad turned back to face them. "Goodbye, Gary," he said. "Goodbye, Clara."

"C'mon, Clara. I'll race you to the gate," Gary said, taking off in a sprint.

"So have you met that guy before?" he asked, once they had both arrived, winded, at the cemetery gate.

"No, I haven't."

"You don't have your name written on any of your clothing, do you?" Gary asked.

"No. I stopped doing that when I was five."

"Okay, this is going to sound dumb, but I am absolutely positive," Gary said, "that we never told him your name."

It didn't sound dumb. It sounded creepy. Gary was right.

Something else occurred to Clara.

"Gary...I think he had a black eye."

"No, I would have noticed. I couldn't stop looking at his eyes because they were two different colors."

"And those two different colors were?"

"One was blue and the other one...oh my gosh, I'm so dumb."

"Yeah. We've been thinking about this wrong."

"It was black. He didn't have a quote-unquote black eye, he had, literally, a *black eye.*"

"He could be the cursed one. He never took off his glove. What if he has a horn for a hand? What do you think that means? Like a hand made of keratin or something?"

Gary shook his head. "Oh, oh wait—no. I think it's something else. Some of the old folks around here use *hand* as a slang word for a name. Like it's short for *handle.* My grandpa used to say, *What's your hand?* when he started forgetting who people were."

"Tad Trumpeter? A horn? Oh," Clara said. "A *horn*. Trum-peter."

"I think we just met the Baneful and Cursed One."

They both glanced uneasily back at the man on the exca-vator. *Just what was this man capable of doing?* Clara wondered, biting her lip.

13

C lara had science homework to do, and a list of important European literary works to memorize for the scholastic bowl team, but the most important assignment, she felt, was the one she had given herself. She and Gary had decided that each of them should undertake a little information-gathering mission. Gary's job was to find out everything he could about the special enchantment-detecting artifact that Constance Love had alluded to in the book, the location of which was still a mystery. He was also supposed to look into Tad Trumpeter and his excavation business.

Clara's job was to find out the true bloodline of Constance Love. She was certain now that she and Constance were related, but she didn't know the specifics. More important, she didn't know how many other blood relatives of Constance Love might also be alive. Clara was an only child, and as far as she knew, she didn't have any cousins. She used to be jealous of kids with big families. It had always been just Clara and her mom. The only thing she knew about her father was that he had never been a part of the picture.

Clara put her textbooks aside. Chemistry could wait. Her mother was off work tonight, which was rare for a school night, and Clara wanted to ask her about their family history. Her mom didn't talk much about Clara's grandmother and never talked about Clara's father at all.

Clara found her mom reading a mystery novel in the den.

"I've got this *family tree* assignment, Mom," Clara improvised. "I just have to pick one side and go back as far as I can. I figure ours will be interesting because we're from here, aren't we?"

"Oh, I'm terrible at remembering family stuff, hon," her

mom said. "But your grandmother wrote everything down in her bible. Let's see if we can find that."

Twenty minutes later Clara had her matrilineal heritage neatly mapped out.

In 1997, thirteen years ago, Clara was born to Cecilia Hutchins. Unmarried, Cecilia Hutchins kept her father's last name. She had been born in 1971 in Biskopskulla to Catherine Hutchins, who had married Walter in the late 1950s.

Catherine Hutchins's maiden name was Anderson. She was born in 1928, the daughter of Carrie Anderson. Carrie had married John Anderson, another descendant of Biskopskulla's settlers, and they had both lived in Biskopskulla their entire lives.

Carrie Anderson's mother's married name, confusingly, was *also* Carrie Anderson, because she had wed a man named James Anderson before giving birth to a daughter in 1894. James Anderson was no relation to his son-in-law John Anderson. It appeared there were only so many surnames to go around among the early Swedish immigrant community in Illinois, Clara thought.

Carrie Anderson the First was born Carrie Olofsson in 1870. Her father, Carl Olofsson, was one of the original settlers of Biskopskulla, brought by his parents to Illinois when he was just a little boy. Carrie Olofsson's mother was Mary Olofsson, or Mary Love before she'd married—the sister of Constance Love.

At least, that's what was written on the genealogy page of the enormous family bible. Clara, however, had a contradictory source—an article by a historian named Regina Farber, published in an Illinois history magazine that she'd photocopied in the school library. Regina Farber had written of strong circumstantial evidence that Biskopskulla's famous so-called witch had given birth to a child during the three-month period in which she'd mysteriously disappeared. The official version of events, believed by most historians, was that Constance Love spent the three months in Chicago, to avoid the fierce condemnation of the religious community she'd been born into. Constance Love had always been unpopular with children her age, and rumors surrounded her as she grew to be a young woman. Contemporary accounts described the selflessness of Constance's sister, Mary, and her efforts to protect her younger sister.

Regina Farber referenced a letter written by Constance to Mary, with a return address in Springfield, Illinois, as well as records from the Springfield Library from the town's 1870 hotel registry where a woman named Mary Olofsson signed in for a stay of several nights—exactly four months later. Although both "Mary" and "Olofsson" were common names, the signature on the registry, Regina argued, was further evidence that Constance Love had given birth to a child before returning to Biskopskulla and subsequently being tried for witchcraft.

Clara now had a list of all the women in her family, dating back to 1870.

And with that, she had a pretty clear idea who her great-great-great-grandmother was.

When she called Gary to tell him what she'd found out, he was too excited to listen.

"You're not going believe what *I* found out!" he said, "But I know what we need to do next."

"What did you find?" Clara asked.

"I went through all the books of local lore that my mom has, and I sorted them based on which I think is the most credible. Based on how close the author was to the people they were writing about. Man, there are a lot of really boring books about witchcraft."

"That's surprising."

"But there's one book that has information we can use. I found a book about local legends written by someone who actually knew what they were talking about, and I think he actually makes a reference to Constance Love. So I'm going to read that one first."

"That's great!"

"But the most important thing is…" Gary trailed off. "Hang on. I think there's someone at the door."

Clara kept holding her phone until she heard a loud thud in her ear.

"Sorry," Gary said, his voice distant. "Dropped my phone." Clara heard the sound of a tinny rattling sound, then a long pause, before Gary returned to the phone. "I can't see from here. I thought someone knocked on the door or something. I'll call you right back." He hung up.

He didn't call back.

14

The next day, Clara found Gary at his locker and punched his arm.

"Ow?" Gary said.

"Don't say you'll call me back if you're not going to call me back!"

"I got hungry," Gary said. "I had to make a sandwich. I figured I'd see you today."

"Well, I was worried," she said. "You thought you heard someone, and then you disappeared."

"Oh, that's...thoughtful of you. But you're not in the big city anymore. This place is a lot safer than Orange County."

"Maybe before the Cursed and Baneful One was on the loose."

"True."

"But you were about to tell me something important?" The first-period bell rang. Clara realized the hallway was nearly empty.

"I'll tell you later," Gary called over his shoulder as he ran to class.

In second period, Gary showed up at the library with a few other students from his English class. "We're doing research for a paper about Shakespeare, but I don't care. I just want to show you something on the computer."

They drew up chairs at one of the library computers and Gary opened a browser. "Here's what I found," Gary said. "Trumpeter Excavation has a website. It's pretty janky. Look."

Clara saw a business web page that could charitably be described as minimal. *T. Trumpeter Excavation & Demolition* scrolled across the top in block letters. Below that a phone number and fax number were listed.

"Do people still use fax machines?" Clara wondered.

"Old people."

"Yeah."

The website featured a cartoonish picture of an excavator on top of a tacky brick background image that covered the whole page. At the bottom were two links. One said "email" and the other said "reviews."

"Read the reviews," Gary urged.

There was a grand total of three reviews. "Trumpeter does great work for a great price!" said the first review. "A good guy that doesn't cut any corners," read the second one. "No complaints—did the job with no fuss," was the third.

"Well, at least he has satisfied customers," Clara pointed out.

"Look at the dates," Gary advised.

Each review was stamped with a date and location. Deer Grove, Wisconsin, May 7, 2005. Fort Monroe, Iowa, October 1, 2007. Bardtown, Kentucky, April 2, 2009.

"Notice anything funny about those towns?" Gary asked.

It took Clara a while to realize it. "DG!" she said, remembering the strange list of letters and numbers in Constance Love's book. "FM! And Bardtown could very well be abbreviated BT."

"Right."

"So we're just missing SC? What does it mean?"

"Well, I looked into it. Remember the numbers?"

"Yeah." Clara opened her backpack and took out the notebook where she'd copied some of the text from the book, including the page with the cryptic abbreviations.

"DG 5

FM 19

SC 12

BT 21"

"Are you ready for this?" Gary asked. From his back pocket he pulled some articles he'd printed off the internet.

He'd circled a few sentences with a highlighter. "I started looking at newspapers for those towns on those particular dates, just to see if something popped up. Look at this." He smoothed open the pages so Clara could see the newspaper headlines clearly.

A tank truck carrying 7500 gallons of chlorine overturned on highway 80 near Dear Grove, killing 5 people and injuring scores of others.

A fire at the Fort Monroe Hospital on Wednesday left 15 patients and 4 hospital staff members dead.

Tornado Outbreak Kills 21 in Bardtown.

Clara felt sick. "Five people died in Deer Grove. Nineteen in Fort Monroe—"

"And twenty-one in Bardtown." Gary finished her sentence. "And who knows? Maybe Trumpeter worked in a town with the initials SC but nobody felt like leaving a review."

"*Unnatural Calamities*, that was the heading in Constance's book. So he could have caused the crash and the fire, but how could anyone cause a tornado? It's hardly an unnatural calamity, is it?"

"Well, who knows what kind of power a witch can wield, right? Maybe the tornado was caused by some kind of enchantment. It says here in the article that meteorologists were taken by surprise. I think Constance could tell that some bad things were going to happen, but she didn't know exactly what."

"She predicted one more calamity. In Biskopskulla," Clara said softly.

"Not a calamity," Gary corrected, "a cataclysm."

"These…calamities…killed fifty-seven people in towns that Tad Trumpeter visited. I'd hate to see what happens if a cataclysm occurs."

Gary looked up at his classmates, who were preparing to leave the library. "We have to stop him. I'll tell you the rest of the stuff I figured out in seventh period."

In art class Gary took a seat next to Clara. Clara was working on her ink sketch of her great-grandmother. At the other end of the table Chris was bent over a drawing of his own. "We have a mission, Clara. A quest. And we were chosen for it," Gary whispered in Clara's direction.

Clara pressed her lips together. At the moment, she was focused more on the ominous threat that made their "quest" necessary.

"So what's this stuff you figured out?" Clara whispered back.

"Okay, so there are lots of different books about witch-craft," Gary said. "And there are quite a few books about Biskopskulla. I've been looking through them to find out everything I can. But the one that seems most promising isn't written by an American at all. It's an English translation of a Swedish book about witches in Illinois. It doesn't mention Biskopskulla by name, but it does refer to a 'Witch Named Love,' who might be our girl."

"Our girl?"

"You know what I mean. The author's name is Olle Gardell. He wrote these books—children's books, basically—in the early 1970s. It was like a series of books about local legends. They were meant to be nonfiction, but sort of scary for kids. The weird thing is that he seemed to choose the places he wrote about completely at random. He wrote a book about lore of the New Hebrides islands, and Quito in Ecuador, and the Westfjords in Iceland. Not all of Iceland, though—just a whole book about one peninsula there."

"That's sort of interesting. In a boring sort of way."

"I know, right? So the only one of his books my mom has is the one about Illinois. It's a collection of local legends, but a few of them are really spot on. Most importantly, it says the Witch Named Love wrote books—more than one of them—and that these books have been missing since the 1910s."

"Books, plural?"

"Yes, so, at least two. But get this: her first book was locked inside a wooden box, after she died. Olle Gardell doesn't say how he knows this, but he's very specific: Book. Locked. In a box. And then someone hid it away, and it hasn't been seen again."

"Or at least it hadn't been seen at the time when he was writing these books."

"Right."

"Well, there's one more book we need to find. I wish he knew where it was."

"Tell me about it," said Gary. "But there's something else I think we should look for first. Olle describes a magical artifact called the Häxa Stone. Apparently, it has been in Biskopskulla for centuries, even before it was settled. It detects enchantments."

"Just like the one Constance referred to. They must both be referring to the same artifact!"

"Yeah, that's what I thought too," Gary whispered. "The legend is that the stone actually doomed Constance Love. Like it was used at her trial to prove she was magic, or cursed, or whatever she was. It's supposed to have been sort of famous among witches, even though its exact location has been lost for years. Like, traveling witches would visit it."

"Visit it? How big is it?"

"Pretty big. Supposed to be about the size of a coffin. Olle says it's somewhere in the woods.

"And if we find it," Clara interjected excitedly, "maybe it will help us find her bones. But it sounds like it's not something we can carry around."

"Well, first we have to find it," Gary said, "but there are literally thousands of acres of woods around here."

"I'd like to read this book."

"I figured. I have it in my locker."

Chris then slid his chair down the table until his seat was directly beside Clara.

"We're kinda busy, Chris. No offense," Gary said.

"You guys are looking for the Häxa Stone?" Chris asked. He pronounced it like *hack-saw*.

"We're just talking about a paper we have to write for our English class," Gary said. "Local legends, and all that."

"I have really good ears, man," Chris said, continuing to work on his drawing.

"It's not a big deal," Gary said, in a voice that suggested it was, in fact, a very big deal.

"I understand," Chris said, not looking up. "You don't want anyone to think you're crazy."

"Shut up, Chris," Gary said.

"That's a yes."

Clara put her pen down. "Have you heard of the Häxa Stone, Chris?"

"Maybe," Chris said. "My grandma. She was into that stuff."

"Was she a witch?" Clara asked.

"Well, she was into it. That doesn't mean she was one. I mean, I'm into samurai stuff, but that doesn't make me a samurai," Chris said. "Yet." He continued. "She talked about the Häxa Stone, and how it would glow at night during rituals. I mean, like in olden times. The fifties and sixties."

"Did she tell you where it was?" Clara asked.

"Nah. But I found it in the woods when I was a kid."

"Did it glow?"

"Once it did."

Gary grunted, annoyed. "What did it look like?" he asked.

"Big rock. Shaped like a coffin."

"You already heard me say that!" Gary said. "You haven't seen it. Shut up."

"Whatever," Chris said. "S'what I get for trying to be helpful."

"Do you know where it is?" Clara asked. "Like, if you had to find it?"

"Yeah," Chris said. "It was my secret place for a while. I used to go there sometimes when my dad...when I didn't feel like hanging out at home."

Gary pinched Clara's knee under the table.

"Then I got bored with it," Chris continued. "I tried to dig it up, but it was too big. I found a really cool skeleton buried at one end of it, though."

Clara dropped her paintbrush. She couldn't hide her excitement. "You found a skeleton?"

"Oh no, not like that. It was a cat skeleton," Chris said.

"That's right," Gary said, drawing in a sharp breath. "That's absolutely right. Olle Gardell talked about a ritual... they buried a cat at the foot of the Häxa Stone. A live cat."

"He looked pretty dead when I found him," Chris said.

Gary put his hand on Chris's shoulder. "Chris," he said. "Buddy. You have to keep this a secret. It's really important."

"Because you guys are on a quest?" Chris said.

"Yeah," Gary said. "It's...a lot to explain. But you have to show me and Clara where this stone is. It's important. Like, life-or-death important."

"Gary," Chris said. "Buddy. I don't *have* to do anything."

Clara felt crestfallen. Finding the stone by themselves seemed an impossible feat. She tried to think of something to say.

"But I *want* to," Chris finished with a grin. "'Bout time something interesting happened around here. When do we start?"

15

That night, Clara dreamt of terrible things. She was walking through the village in a thunderstorm. Lightning was flashing in the distance, and some of the buildings were on fire, but no one seemed to notice.

Throngs of people walked the streets—her teachers, Mrs. Maynard, the Mahlers, and strangers too—they all looked straight ahead and kept walking, dangerously close to the burning structures.

"Stop!" she shouted, but no one seemed to be able to hear her.

She saw her classmates, oblivious to the rain, the lightning, and the fires. Kaitlyn, Edison, Myron, Gary, and Chris—and other students whose names she didn't know.

"The bell!" she thought. "I'll ring the bell to warn them!" But when she ran to the church, she found it had already burned down. Nothing remained but a smoldering shell. The church bell had fallen and lay on its side, useless, in front of the charred front steps.

Clara heard a noise.

The tomb beside the church was still intact, its door shaking. Something was trying to get out.

A man walked right in front of the tomb. It was Raymond Bergstrom, wearing his three disheveled sweatshirts. She shouted at him to warn him, then remembered that no one could hear her. Raymond Bergstrom looked up at her, locked his eyes upon hers, and put a finger over his mouth.

Then, with a loud thunderclap, a bolt of lightning struck him, and Clara woke with a start.

Disquieted, she re-read a passage she'd discovered in the book borrowed from Gary, the book by Olle Gardell. It wasn't a passage about Constance Love, or about the Häxa Stone.

She turned to the book's appendix, past the glossary. She scanned the odd-sounding terms. *"Animism:* belief that objects, places, and living things are all possessed of distinct spiritual essence…*Bibliomancy:* use of books for divination…. *Distaff line:* the mother's bloodline within a family…"

The next section, labeled "Magical Objects Seen in Henry County," was full of small black-and-white illustrations with handwritten captions. A nail bent in two directions. Painted pebbles. A stuffed toad.

Clara fingered the charm she wore around her neck. It was the necklace she'd found while cleaning up her grandmother's things. She'd thought at the time it was a rather plain butterfly necklace, and she had worn it a few times. But it wasn't a butterfly. It was a moth.

She was looking at a life-sized drawing of it in Olle Gardell's book, published sometime in the 1970s.

"The moth charm brings luck," Gardell had written, "wards off diseases of the eye. On rare occasions, it can even mend a broken heart."

Where had her grandmother found the necklace? What was it doing in an envelope in a shoebox? Why were there so many legends in Biskopskulla?

It took her a long time to get back to sleep.

16

Clara knocked on Gary's front door.

"I brought bagels," she said, holding up a bag when he opened the door.

They ate fresh bagels with raspberry jam in the Mahler's breakfast nook.

"Does Chris really live in a junkyard?" Clara asked between bites.

"Yes. Well, he doesn't live *in* the junkyard. He lives right next to it. His dad helps run it."

"That must not help his popularity at school."

"Yeah, kinda sucks. But it's not like he needs help to be unpopular. He could live in a mansion and he'd probably still be weird."

"Have you guys been in the same class since kindergarten?"

"Yeah. Most of us have. A couple kids got held back, and we got a couple kids added to our class when they were held back from the class ahead of us, but for the most part, it's all the same people."

"It must be cool to know everybody that well."

"It would be, if you cared about everybody. But there are lots of people that you just aren't that interested in, you know? I don't mean that in a mean way," he said.

Gary's dad was working, even though it was Saturday. His mom was shopping. It dawned on Clara that they were not, in fact, getting a ride to the junkyard.

They packed sandwiches into her backpack, carefully sealing them into freezer bags to protect the book—Constance Love's book—that Clara had brought today, just in case they needed to consult it while they were out. "Are we seriously walking there? How far is it? Why do people walk every-where around here?"

Gary shrugged. "It's walking distance."

"That term takes on whole new meanings in rural America."

At this, Gary smiled. "Fifteen minutes, tops."

According to Clara's cell phone, fifteen was closer to twenty-five. Finally they arrived at Chris's house, marked by a roadside mailbox with the name BECK painted on its side. Chris was in his front yard, working on an upside-down bike that looked like it had survived several different presidential administrations. An extra-large red T-shirt hung off his skinny frame, and his baggy jeans looked two sizes too big.

"Hola, amigos!" he shouted as the two visitors approached, putting down his work and taking a few running steps in their direction.

"Hi, Chris," Clara said, warmly.

Chris took them by the shoulders conspiratorially. "You want to see a dead coyote?" He looked genuinely excited, and Clara was struck by the way his long hair gleamed gold in the sun. I wouldn't mind having hair like that, she thought wistfully.

"No, I think I'm full up on seeing dead things for the day. But thanks," she said.

"That sounds *awesome*, actually," Gary said.

Chris led them into his house, a dilapidated structure whose peeling paint revealed wood that had turned gray.

"The dead coyote is in *here*?" she asked, aghast. Chris rolled his eyes.

"Well, yeah. It'd get all gross if we left it outside." He opened a door to the basement. Clara noticed that, like one of the doors in her grandmother's home, the knob was home to dozens of mismatched rubber bands. She figured it must be a small-town thing.

"Watch the fourth step," Chris cautioned, sprinting down

a set of rickety wooden stairs to the basement. Clara count-ed—one, two, three, four—and avoided the step, making her way much more carefully toward the bottom. Gary followed her. *Crack!* The wood beneath her feet made a sudden splin-tering sound and she found herself lurching forward. She shrieked, as Chris, moving surprisingly gracefully, caught her.

"I meant the fourth step from the bottom," he explained. Gary laughed, stepping gingerly around the broken step.

At the bottom of the staircase was a large chest freezer, the biggest Clara had ever seen. This must come in handy in a town where the nearest supermarket is thirty miles away, she thought. Chris lifted the lid and a dim light emerged.

"Check it, check it," he said. Inside, atop stacks of white-wrapped butcher packages and brick-like plastic bags of frozen vegetables, a small coyote lay curled on its side. One of its legs stuck out at an odd angle, and Clara couldn't see whether its eyes were open or closed.

"Cool," Gary offered.

"I know, right?" said Chris.

Clara felt a little sick. "So, uh, are you guys are going to *eat* it?"

Gary laughed and Chris made a face. "Aw, no! Coyotes taste awful! You can get a bounty on their pelts for part of the year, though. People who hit little fellas like this on the road probably don't know that, or they'd have kept him themselves."

"Why do you have him in the freezer then?"

"Because it's the wrong time of year. There's no bounty yet."

As they climbed back up the stairs, Clara made a mental note not to eat meat at the Becks' house. Or vegetables. Or anything else. Ever.

Clara's cell phone beeped twice. Her mother was texting to see if she would be home in time for dinner. She replied Yes, and then Chris reached for her phone.

"Is that a touch-screen phone? Can I see it?"

Clara reluctantly let him take the phone.

"Check this out," Chris said, opening up a new text message. He lifted the phone so that the screen's keyboard was just an inch from his face, then quickly stuck out his tongue three times. He handed the phone back to her.

"Gross," she said. On the screen Chris had typed "LOL" with his tongue. The keyboard display was slightly shiny with his spit.

"Nice," Gary said expressionlessly. "Funny thing is, you wouldn't be able to do that if your tongue were lolling."

The other two just stared at him. "Man," said Chris, "I thought *my* jokes were bad."

"So you really, really believe that the Häxa Stone is in here?" Clara asked as they walked through the junkyard. "You're not just having fun?"

"Aw, heck yeah," Chris said, "this place wasn't always a trash heap. A hundred years ago, this was the edge of town, and this is where they used to have secret meetings. For the religious cult. Ask Gary! His mom knows all about the spooky crap."

Gary shrugged. "Supposedly, there used to be a meeting place about half a mile from here. This place is too far out to include on the walking tour, though."

"That's right, about half a mile," Chris said. "But that was for the cult. This was for the cult inside the cult, it's even deeper back."

Clara had never been in a junkyard before, unless you counted the apartment she and her mom had lived in for a few months when she was nine. "This place is bigger than I expected."

"It takes space. This place is mostly old cars and run-down farm equipment, big stuff." Indeed, it looked like a graveyard for outdated machinery. If machines had souls, what kind of hauntings would take place here? Clara wondered. It was a thought that might seem silly during the day, but would have been eerie in the dark.

They walked to the very edge of the junkyard and then into the woods. They kept walking for a long time. Eventually Chris brought them to a depression in the ground with two thick-trunked trees growing in it.

"Here we go," he said, brushing dirt and leaves aside to reveal a huge, flat slab of stone next to one of the trees. "The Häxa Stone. No one else knows where it is."

"Are you sure this is it?" Clara asked. It looked so plain. She had expected something with carvings, runes...anything but this flat gray mass. It was about five feet from one end to the other, and roughly coffin shaped. It barely stuck out of the ground, so she couldn't tell how deeply the bottom of it was buried.

"It's legit. This is where they brought Constance Love for her trial. They laid her on the rock, and when it glowed, they knew she was a witch."

"How did they know in advance that the rock could tell if she was a witch? That doesn't make sense," Clara asked with a frown.

"Maybe Erik Mattsson told them it would. When you're in a cult, you don't really question the guy in charge."

Gary squatted next to the stone. "It looks like any old rock."

Clara sat down next to him. "It's a shame it isn't smaller. Something we could hold up next to Tad to see if he's evil."

"Not evil," Gary corrected. "Enchanted."

"How do you know this is the rock, Chris?"

Chris leaned against the tree and folded his arms. "You think I made it up? Aw, heck no. When I was a kid, my grandma was this old crazy lady. I mean, seriously. She was like twenty years older than my grandpa, and he was almost eighty. And she grew up in this shack, okay? Just this one-room shanty with a bunch of other kids, and she never had a job in her life. She just did favors for people."

"What kind of favors?" Gary asked.

"She did magic. She would hex people for you, or she would help your crops grow. Crazy. She used to do this blessing over me every time I would ride my bike or go skating, and I never got injured. Not seriously, anyway."

"Did she come out here? Did she ever see this rock?"

"No, but she—see, my dad needed to dig a new well out here when I was a kid. Our well had too much iron in it."

"Doesn't that damage your brain?" Gary asked.

"No," he said. "No, I don't believe it does, Gary. It's just bad for you."

"Sorry. Just asking."

"Anyway, Grandma thought we would need help finding a good spot for a well. So she sent Dad a dowsing rod, one that she had made. Do you know what that is?"

"Of course," Gary said. "Everybody knows what that is, right, Clara?"

Clara was pretty sure she could guess what it was, even if she couldn't have spelled it. "Isn't that a stick that helps you find water?"

"Exactamundo," Chris said, touching his nose. "Dad threw it out. He said it was crap. But I dug it out of the garbage because it was the perfect shape to make a slingshot. I almost killed a bobcat with that thing once," he said, proudly. "Anyway. I was out here one day, and I was shooting at cans and stuff when I was a kid, and I set my slingshot down on this rock and it got warm. Like, really warm. The rest of the rock was cold, and where the dowsing rod touched it, it was warm. Pretty cool, huh?"

Clara felt disappointed. She'd been hoping for something more conclusive, some reason to believe the rock they were sitting near was something more than a rock.

"Was it a sunny day?" Gary asked. "What time was it?

Where was the sun in the sky? Is it possible the tree here was creating a shadow on the rest of the rock, so it only seemed like the dowsing rod made it hot?"

Chris shrugged. "I don't remember if it was sunny. But no, it's not possible, because I know what I saw. The slingshot made contact with the rock here. And then I felt it. I moved it to another part of the rock, and it got warm, almost hot, and it got warm in a Y-shaped pattern. So that's how I know."

"Did you show anybody else?" Clara asked, leaning back against the side of the rock, her backpack providing a nice cushion after their long walk.

"No. I didn't want to get in trouble for digging the stick out of the trash."

"Where is the stick now?" Gary asked.

Chris shrugged. "It was a long time ago. I lost it."

"Did you ever test it to see if it could really find water?" Gary asked.

"Not really. I mean, we had water. I didn't really need it."

"If I had a real dowsing rod," Gary continued, "I would put it through a series of tests to see if it actually worked. But no one has ever been proven to actually be able to do that—to find water with any more success than chance."

"I don't know about proven, but my grandma could do it, before she died."

"She thought she could do it," Gary corrected. "That doesn't mean she actually could."

"Yeah, but then the stone proved her stick was magic."

"I'm sorry, Chris," Gary said in a condescending tone. "I don't think we can just jump to that conclusion. I don't think you have any idea where the Häxa Stone is. I think you just told us about this and brought us out here because you like to hear yourself talk."

"Gary—" Clara protested.

"Well then, Gary," Chris said. "How do you explain *that?*"

Gary looked over at Clara and his eyes widened and his

mouth dropped open. "Clara," he said, in a shocked whisper, "look behind you."

"What?" she asked, sitting upright.

"No, take off your backpack," Gary ordered, reaching to help. He lowered it to the surface of the stone.

As the backpack, which held Constance Love's journal, got closer to the top of the stone, a whirl of particles whipped up in a miniature tornado, as if a hidden wind were blowing from somewhere deep within the rock.

And where the stone came into contact with the backpack, it glowed.

The bright yellow light coming from deep within the rock was unlike anything Clara had ever seen before.

17

Chris, Gary, and Clara sat on the green shag carpet in Clara's basement. Gary took out a scratched rock. It was Chris's first time at Clara's house, and her mom had made tuna salad sandwiches to mark the occasion.

The three of them had spent a considerable amount of time arguing over the Häxa Stone, but ultimately they decided that the relic was useless to them if it wasn't portable. Using a pickaxe retrieved from his house, Chris chipped off a corner, and a hunk of the Häxa Stone fell at their feet.

They tested their new portable Häxa Stone by touching it to Constance's book, and they were happy to see that it glowed brightly. This seemed to prove Gary's theory that Constance had somehow enchanted the book in order to better see what happened to it in the future.

Then they had the idea to use the stone to check Clara's moth charm. And indeed, a faint glow could be seen when the moth rested against the stone.

"The moth charm brings luck," Gary said in a fake British accent. "Wards off diseases of the eye. On rare occasions, it can even mend a broken heart."

"That'll be really useful the next time there's a pinkeye outbreak at school," Chris offered with a grin. "Or if you have a really bad crush on a guy who's out of your league."

"Guys, come on," Clara said.

They decided it was important for Chris to read the prediction book. He was a part of their team now, on the quest with them. He seemed to have an opinion about everything, even the minor details. "Okay, yeah," he said to himself. "Buckwheat pancakes are good."

Gary had gone through all of his mother's collection of

local lore and witchcraft books, and he'd made a list of books that he thought they should find. Several of them were by Olle Gardell, the author who had described the Häxa Stone so accurately.

Clara looked at the titles on his list. "These seem kind of obscure."

"Tell me about it," Gary said. "I couldn't find any of them in the school library, or the Gävle Public Library. I looked online, and there is exactly one that I can get through inter-library loan."

"Ugh," Clara said.

"Fortunately, we live in a glorious technotopia. You can buy most of these books used online. But it'll cost about $100." He made a face. "I have a twenty-dollar gift card that I was supposed to spend on books anyway."

"I have some money I made selling dolls."

"Uh, Clara Hutchins, doll vendor extraordinaire. I like that." Gary grinned.

Chris looked up from the book. "I don't have any money, but I am not opposed to doing dishes or stealing things."

"I don't think that'll be necessary, man," Gary said, clapping him on the shoulder. "I can persuade my dad to help pay for one of those as a Christmas gift for Mom."

"Okay, we'll save that option for the future," Chris said. "Speaking of stealing things...I'd like to take our Häxa pebble home for a couple nights."

Clara had been hanging on to their piece of the stone. "What for?"

"I want to check everything in my house for magic. I mean, duh."

Gary nodded. "I actually think that's a good idea. We should all do that, but Chris should start. He's the one who knew where the stone was in the first place, and he says his grandma knew something about witchcraft. I...I can't believe I'm saying this, but I believe him."

18

They sat in a booth at the closest thing Biskopskulla had to a coffee shop: the Biskopskulla Bakery & Eatery, one of two restaurants in town. The other restaurant, the Old Settlers Inn, was located in a historic building, served a menu of nineteenth-century food, and kept an erratic schedule. The Bakery & Eatery was more casual, with furniture that looked only decades old, not centuries.

Clara Hutchins, Gary Mahler, and Chris Beck: they were an unlikely trio, Clara thought, as they each tried to finish up that week's schoolwork in silence. Gary initially had his doubts about Chris's reliability, and Clara still didn't know quite what to make of him, but he seemed as trustworthy as he was weird.

And to be honest, it had felt good to tell another person about everything. Clara wasn't used to keeping secrets, especially not big ones, although she got the sense that Gary had more experience in that area. He never said anything good about his dad, and even though he got along with his mom well enough, he seemed to view his parents as adversaries, a mindset that Clara had never really understood.

Chris, on the other hand, almost never mentioned his father. Clara had gleaned that his mother was gone. He had older brothers, although from what she'd heard they didn't sound like the type of guys who helped nurture their younger sibling. If anything, Clara thought, Chris seemed a little feral to her, like a wolf or cat who'd just raised himself in the vicinity of his family.

"It's crazy how long you can go without cutting your toenails, you know?" Chris said suddenly.

"No," Clara said. "I didn't know that. I really didn't."

Gary looked up from his book and then looked down quickly, trying hard to suppress a snicker. He was almost successful, until he heard Chris giggle, and then the two of them were laughing together, almost like friends.

Clara smiled. It was an unexpected turn of events.

Once homework was done—or once at least two thirds of it was finished, which was Gary's personal quota—the three discussed their situation. Now that Chris knew their secret, Gary thought it necessary to stress to him why they weren't planning to involve anyone else in their mission: Not only was there a strong chance they wouldn't be believed, but their one adult "ally," Constance Love, had specifically warned them against it. This all seemed perfectly reasonable to Chris, who made it a habit never to tell adults anything that might make sense to them.

The next item of business was to figure out how to tackle the tasks ahead of them. Gary wanted to see if Tad Trumpeter was using any enchanted objects in his contracting business. If he was looking for the body of Constance Love, did he have a magical advantage? Clara thought this was foolish—she had no desire to be anywhere near Tad Trumpeter again.

Chris pulled their piece of the Häxa Stone out of his pocket and handed it to Gary. "Apparently, magic is not all that common. I seriously checked every object in every room except my brother's locked bedroom, and I'm pretty sure that just has a bed and a suitcase of DVDs. But it never lit up. Not at the books, not at any antiques we found in the dump, not even at the arrowheads and tomahawks my dad collected."

"That's too bad," Gary said.

"Right? I would *love* a magic weapon!"

Clara wanted to develop a plan to search the junkyard. Her thinking was that if the Haxa Stone was near there, and given that the junkyard had been the meeting place for cult groups, they might find the rest of what they were looking for nearby. Chris liked this idea, mostly because it would give him a chance to show off his knowledge of the junkyard. Gary, however, was adamant that this wasn't how these things worked; you never find two of your quest items in the same location.

"This isn't a video game, Gary. This is real life," Clara said.

"Video game tropes are based on archetypes," Gary said. "There's a reason these myths are so common in the human psyche." Clara nodded in slow motion.

Just then, Raymond Bergstrom stormed into the Biskopskulla Bakery & Eatery. He was wearing the same stained sweatpants that he'd worn on the day of the Hawley Douglas 5K. This time, instead of a belt, he had looped several feet of nylon clothesline around his waist. His T-shirt was huge, a size too large even for his bulky frame, and it depicted a fat Santa Claus on his sleigh wearing a cowboy hat, with the slogan "Everything's Bigger in Texas!" in large block letters.

"Can I help you?" the cafe owner's daughter, who served as both waitress and cook on weekdays, asked him.

"The children," he said. "I'm looking for the children—"

He saw Clara, Gary, and Chris out of the corner of his eye and spun around.

"You children!" he shouted. "Two...no, three?"

With an uneven gait, he walked over to their table.

"Ah, yes," Raymond Bergstrom said, "three of you. Here today. Biskopskulla kids doing st-st-studying. Biskopsk-skulla. Here today. Gone tomorrow."

To Clara, it seemed as though he wasn't so much talking *to* the three of them as talking to himself. Once he got close to them, he avoided eye contact, choosing to look into the space between their heads.

"Is everything okay?" Clara asked, although she was pretty sure that if there were any mental health services to be had in a town this size, they would have already been offered to this man.

Bergstrom ignored her. "Like Krakatoa."

"Crack a toe?" Chris asked.

"Don't engage," Gary admonished him.

Bergstrom paid them no mind. "Krakatoa," he said. "Eighteen eighty-three. An explosion of overwhelming pr-pr-pro-portions. Eleven cubic miles of ash. Waves a hundred feet high. Thousands dead. Thousands upon thousands. Dead."

"He's talking about the volcano in Krakatoa," Gary said.

"I know," said Clara, who had not actually known.

"Volcano, but—" Bergstrom continued, "but there were children. Like you, it always st-st-st-st—"

He seemed stuck, so Clara suggested, "Starts?"

"Stops?" Gary offered.

"Stitches?" Chris said.

Bergstrom suddenly looked like he didn't know where he was. "Starts, stops, stitches, witches."

"What about witches?" Clara asked, intrigued.

Bergstrom didn't look at her. "I don't know anything about witches," he said, "and neither should you. Bah!" He slapped an imaginary fly on his neck, and Clara flinched. "There's no such thing anyways."

He turned around as if to walk away, but then he turned back to them.

"They're after me," he said. "They're after me. And if they get me, they'll get you. And if they get you?"

"Um, what?" said Clara.

"Boom. Like Kraka—Krakatoa."

He shuffled toward the door, muttering to himself.

Clara called after him, "Do you need any help?"

"Bah!" he said. "Do *you* need any help."

It was a weird encounter, but they soon forgot about it, for as their eyes followed Raymond Bergstrom out the door of the Bakery & Eatery, they saw Tad Trumpeter through the cafe's plate-glass window, standing on the sidewalk outside the post office across the street.

He was staring right at them.

19

After the death of their mother, Constance Love lived with her sister, Mary, and Mary's husband, Carl. Their father had died when the girls were young. Mary was the older sister, but in truth the two young women looked like twins, though Mary was three years older than Constance.

Carl worked in one of two flour mills in the area. Although he was not a rich man, he was quiet and kind like his wife, and would never countenance the thought of leaving his sister-in-law to fend for herself. Constance tried to make herself of use to the household, but she was not particularly skilled at homemaking tasks like sewing or cooking.

At gardening, however, she excelled, and the vegetable patch she tended, called a kitchen garden, produced food to eat, to can for the winter, and to trade: lettuce, snap beans, and beets in the spring; squash, onions, and cabbage in the late summer.

Today was midsummer, and Constance was tending to tomato plants that were nearly as tall as her head when a man wearing gloves and a wide-brimmed work hat rode near on a dark horse and dismounted.

"Young lady!" the man called to her, his accent not one she'd heard before. "Do you know of an inn, where a man can eat and rest?"

"There is a lodging house not two miles north along the road you're traveling. You can secure a fine meal there and a comfortable room, I'm sure."

The man nodded, and a gust of wind caught his hat's brim, blowing it off his head to land at the edge of Constance's garden. With some annoyance, she stooped down to retrieve it and handed it back to him.

He was just about to spur his horse onward when Constance dropped the tomato she was holding and looked off into space. Her fingers twitched and she clasped and unclasped her hands a few times, quickly. She cleared her throat and blinked a few times.

"I should say the inn is full. You'll need to ride ten miles north, or find a farmer who will exchange a place to eat and sleep for some hard work."

The man coughed as he took in the girl before him. "Why should you now say that the inn is full?" he asked. "Did someone tell you this? Had you forgotten?"

Constance did not answer directly. "Either way, there are no rooms to let. Good day, sir."

The man narrowed his eyes—his black right eye and pale blue left eye—but said nothing.

20

Regina Farber walked out of the farmhouse with a slice of homemade peach pie wrapped neatly in aluminum foil (or, as Ruth, the kindly nonagenarian woman who owned the house called it, "tinfoil.")

It was the late 1960s, and having earned her graduate degree in history, Regina was engaged in a special project to learn more about the role of women in communities of religious settlers. The specific focus of her research was the women of the Biskopskulla colony.

Of course, by this time all the original settlers, male and female, were dead, so Regina sought out the children and grandchildren of the original settlers who'd struck out from Sweden and braved the harsh winters of Illinois.

Ruth, who owned the farmhouse, had been born in the 1870s and was old enough to remember some of the women who'd followed Erik Mattsson across the ocean and then survived that first harsh winter.

And she was also old enough to have talked about the murder of Constance Love with the very people who'd killed her.

"If my aunt Margaret were alive today, she would swear up and down that she had nothing to do with Constance's death. But she told me one night after half a bottle of cooking sherry that she was there that night, hunting Constance down. Margaret said she helped carry the poor woman to the hanging tree!"

Margaret Allgren, born in 1847, had died in 1938.

"I asked her if she had any regrets," Ruth said. "She said she hated to think on it, what they did to that woman. Constance Love. But they'd all been so sure, back then. The whole town turned up for the hanging. Everyone knew about it. Everyone was so sure she was a witch.'"

Regina opened the passenger side door of her used 1961 Oldsmobile, and a book fell from a stack on the passenger seat onto the gravel driveway. Horrified, Regina picked it up and blew off the dust. Of all the books to drop, this one was the oldest, a book of hymns from the archival collection at the Rock Island Public Library.

She thought she saw dirt smudges on the page, and she blew carefully on it. On closer inspection, she saw that the marks were made by a pencil. Someone had drawn circles above three letters on page eighty-four of this book: a B, and then a few lines below that, an E, and then, near the bottom of the page, an R. On the facing page, Regina saw that an exclamation point had a circle drawn on top of it.

That's odd, she thought. Just last week, she'd encountered similar defacement of an equally old manuscript.

Getting into the car, she reached into the back seat for her briefcase and retrieved a stack of neatly labeled manila folders.

In a matter of seconds, she found the copy she was looking for: two pages from a Swedish book of prayers held in the collection of the Rock Island Public Library.

Regina didn't speak Swedish, although she was considering taking a community college class to learn it, so great was her love of Illinois history. These prayers were special because they had been part of morning services for the Mattssonists in Biskopskulla.

Someone had taken a pencil and drawn harsh marks on the pages containing the prayers. Three dark circles.

Over the letters F, A, and R.

F-A-R last week. B-E-R this week. And an exclamation point.

As if to say: "FARBER!"

Regina Farber shivered. It was coincidence, of course. She

was a rational person, and she didn't believe in signs. She was particularly fond of saying that we can find patterns anywhere if we look for them; historians mustn't read too much into every pattern that they see.

Still, she wrote the letters down on a fresh sheet of notebook paper and stared at them for a long while.

21

Clara's gaze met Tad Trumpeter's across the street. She immediately looked away, then looked back out the window of the Bakery & Eatery to find that he was still standing in the same place, watching her. She saw him tilt his head without breaking eye contact, as if he was studying her. She kicked Gary under the table, but it was unnecessary. All three of them knew he was out there.

"Just act normal," Clara said.

"What are you talking about?" Chris said, standing. "No time like the present."

"WHAT ARE YOU DOING?" Clara whispered loudly.

"It makes sense," Gary said, as he too stood. "We needed to find an excuse to test out our theory by figuring out how to get close to Trumpeter. Well, here he is!"

"This is crazy," said Clara.

"You can stay here if you want," Chris said. "I just think, hey, don't give him the upper hand."

Chris waved at Tad. The man did not wave back; instead, he tilted his head and smiled.

His smile reminded Clara of the lizards she used to find in her old apartment in Orange County. The first few she'd seen had been juveniles, hard to identify because of their small size. Once she mistook one for a cockroach. But then, one summer, she encountered a fully grown adult lizard. A San Diego alligator lizard, she learned after looking it up. She used to think of lizards as members of one of the *cute* species of animals. But when she spotted her first adult alligator lizard hanging from a curtain in the kitchen one Saturday while her mom was at work, her opinion changed. She got a plastic bucket out from under the sink, hoping to brush the animal gently into the bucket so she could safely relocate it outside. But when she got close, she froze. Its tail whipped back and forth like a snake, and it turned its face toward her.

It was tiny, but it looked like a monster, with its leering jaw and its metallic eyes—eyes that seemed to know what you were thinking. It resembled a cross between a poisonous viper and an alligator, and Clara screamed and dropped the bucket. By the time she steeled her nerves and retrieved the bucket, the lizard was gone. She never saw it again, but she wondered every night whether it might be crawling up her bedspread, or having babies in her closet.

She hadn't thought about that lizard in ages, but the smile of Tad Trumpeter brought it to mind. This is what she ruminated on as she reluctantly followed Chris and Gary out of the cafe.

"You're the guy digging up the cemetery, right?" Chris asked, once he'd crossed the street.

"Good afternoon," said Tad Trumpeter. "I've been excavating the road *near* the cemetery, as it happens. And may I add that as a contractor, I'm always delighted to meet…the locals. The excavation business brings one in touch with so many *fascinating* people."

"Thank you!" Chris said, as if this were a compliment.

"As it happens, I have also signed a contract to expand the basement underneath the middle school. Tell me, are you a student there?"

Clara, who had followed the boys across the street, sent an urgent telepathic message to Chris: *Don't give him any information about you!* She had a bad feeling about anything that Tad Trumpeter was trying to find out.

"Yes, indeed I am," said Chris. "Are you?"

"No," Tad said, with eerie sincerity. "It has been a long time since I was a student."

"Where are you from?" Gary asked. "You don't sound like you're from around here. I've lived here my whole life."

"Very observant," Tad said. "I'm from back East. But I put in several bids for work here, because it is so...beautiful. Peaceful. And Biskopskulla has such a rich history."

"Yeah, it's real peaceful," Chris said.

Clara saw that Gary was palming the fragment of the Häxa Stone as he edged closer to Tad.

Clara knew the stone would glow in proximity to something that was enchanted, but her knowledge of enchantments was limited. Would it glow if it touched a witch's skin? How close did it need to be to an enchanted object in order to work?

Then she noticed, curiously, that Tad still wore a glove on his left hand but not his right.

What if he's hiding something? she thought.

So she took action.

Tad's attention was focused on Chris, who'd started talking about local weeds that grew in cemeteries.

Then she gripped Gary's hand—the one holding the stone—in what she figured would look like a friendly gesture. She hoped he would get the hint, and after a moment, he did. He passed the stone to her as discreetly as he could.

"Mr. Trumpeter," she said, "do you have any kids?"

"I don't have any living children," he said, emotionless. It was a frightening thing to hear coming from him. A normal person, Clara thought, wouldn't be so vague.

"Gosh," Clara said. Then she said, "Oh!"—as if she'd just remembered something—"I found a piece of a statue in the cemetery. I was wondering if you know where it goes?"

She reached out to hand him the Häxa Stone, then let it slip through her fingers onto the sidewalk.

Tad stooped down gracefully and retrieved the rock from the pavement.

No sooner did he have it in his grasp, than he tightened his fingers convulsively around it, as if he intended to pulverize the rock in his fist.

He knows, Clara thought. He knows what it is.

"It is good that you brought me this," Tad said, straightening up. He kept his hand tightly clenched around the rock so it was impossible to see if it glowed or not. "This is an important historic artifact. But—you didn't find this in the cemetery, I don't think. Did you?"

He placed the rock inside his shirt pocket, and then snapped the pocket shut.

"Yes, I'm pretty sure we did," Clara said.

"You're pretty sure?" He sounded annoyed. "You *did* find it there, or you're *pretty sure* you found it there? What part of the cemetery? You know…it's a crime to tamper with historic artifacts."

"As it should be," Gary replied in his fake-respectful tone. Clara's eyes were drawn to the front of Gary's green shirt, where she noticed a curious gold patch on his chest, like the reflection of a sunset.

There was a hole in Tad's pocket, and behind it, the stone was shining like a spotlight. Clara gasped and Tad's eyes moved to her, then down to the hole in his pocket.

His demeanor changed entirely.

"Well now. Where are my manners?" Tad said, in an icy imitation of politeness. "It's getting late. May I offer the three of you a ride home?"

"No, thank you," Clara said. "We still have some homework to do."

Tad tsked. "Ah, but the cafe is closed." He snapped his fingers, and as he did so Clara could've sworn that all the lights in the cafe turned off at the same time.

"We're good," Gary said.

"Are you sure?" Tad asked. "You don't want to walk to the Bed and Breakfast in this weather, do you, Clara?" His gloved right hand cracked the knuckles of his left.

"What weather?" said Chris.

Clara felt a drop of rain on her neck.

"The rain, of course."

"We're totally good, sir," Gary said.

"And you, Gary—it's a bit of a jaunt to get to your house on Flower Street, isn't it?" He turned to Chris. "But don't you have it worst of all, young man? You don't want to walk all the way to the junkyard, do you, Mr. Beck?"

"How do you...know where we live?" Clara asked, not sure she wanted to know the answer.

"My dear, you're not the only ones who do their homework."

The three kids took a step back.

"Come," said Tad. "There's room for all three in the cab of my truck. I want to tell you the story of some young people I once knew who interfered with forces they didn't understand."

"No, thank you," Gary said, taking another step backward and pulling both Clara and Chris with him.

"You're going to want to hear the ending," Tad said, his voice losing any pretense of charm. He cracked another knuckle on his gloved hand as the rain started to pour.

"We need to run," Chris said, and it took Clara just a fraction of a second to realize he meant it literally.

The three of them turned and ran, down the street and around the corner. They didn't stop running until they got to Clara's house, where Gary called his mom to ask if Chris could stay at his place that night.

22

A few days later, Clara was grounded.

Just before eight on Tuesday night, Clara's mom had called to check on her, then heard the boys talking in the background.

"What made you think it would be okay to have boys over when I'm not there, Clara?" she'd demanded.

"I didn't think it was a big deal, Mom," Clara had said. "I'm really sorry."

Clara hoped that would be the end of it, but it wasn't.

After her mother got home, they had a sit-down chat, and Clara was grounded for two weeks—no social life, no visitors. Nothing but school.

This represented a real problem for a girl who was working with her friends to avert a life-threatening catastrophe.

On the second morning of her grounding, Clara woke up early and made oatmeal for breakfast. She waited until her mother had downed her first cup of coffee, then asked, "Can I still go to *school* activities, Mom? Mrs. Maynard wants me to study British literature this week at scholastic bowl practice. They are really relying upon me."

"Hm? Okay, that's fine," her mom said. "But straight home afterward."

"Okay. Thanks, Mom. I love you!" Clara said. She kissed her mother and raced out the door before she could change her mind.

Later that day, during art class, she explained her situation.

"You know what this means, don't you?" Gary said to Chris. "You need to join the scholastic bowl team."

Mrs. Maynard was delighted to have Chris join the team. In

their first practice round, Kaitlyn was on a tear. She answered questions about the Pythagorean theorem and the emperor Caligula. "Finally!" she said during the break. "I feel so *vindicated*."

In the second round, there was a question about Japanese ritual suicide. "Seppuku!" Chris shouted out.

"You have to click the buzzer first," Gary told him.

Chris clicked the buzzer and shouted "Seppuku!" again.

After practice, the three of them hung out together on the lawn in front of the school. "It feels like every day I have to stop and adjust my worldview," Clara said. "I mean, one day it's—maybe magic *is* real. The next day it's—maybe there are witches."

"Maybe there are witches," Gary repeated, as if trying the phrase out.

"I've always known that," Chris said, opening a bag of sunflower seeds. He offered them to his companions before digging in.

"For once I actually believe you," Gary said.

"I mean, sure you knew it," Clara said. "But did you really *know* you knew it? Like, right now, if you needed someone to…cast a spell, do you know anyone you could ask who would know how to do it?"

"Well," Chris said, "Tad Trumpeter, probably."

Clara smirked in spite of herself. "But anyone you trust?"

Gary said, "For me, it's like this: Lots of people believe in angels. I mean, *tons* of people. More than half the country, and way more than half the people around here. But there's a big difference between saying, yeah, sure, I believe in angels…and actually walking into your living room and seeing one, sitting on your couch and glowing and turning on the TV by pointing its finger at it."

"I can turn on my TV by pointing a remote at it," Chris said.

"Not the point."

"Arthur C. Clarke wrote, 'Any sufficiently advanced technology is indistinguishable from magic,'" Chris said.

"One day on the scholastic bowl team and he's quoting famous authors."

"That's the power of extra-curricular activities," Chris said.

"Co-curricular," Gary corrected him.

Clara stopped them. "It makes sense, though. I mean, if we saw someone using a remote control and we didn't know how it worked, we could find out how it worked."

"I don't really care, though," Gary said, "as long as it works."

"Right. But you don't have to care," Clara said, "because you already know there are thousands of people who *do* know how it works—a remote control or any other *sufficiently advanced* technology—so if you ever needed to know, you could turn to them." Chris nodded in agreement.

"But I don't know anyone who understands how magic works," Clara continued. "Except maybe Constance Love. But since we've finished every page of her book, we can't ask her questions anymore. Maybe if we get our hands on the second book, we can."

"That's still so trippy. How you could ask questions of a woman who died a hundred forty years ago," Chris said.

"We have one credible source, so far," Clara said.

"Olle Gardell," Gary said.

"We need to read the rest of those books as soon as they arrive," Clara added.

Chris spat a sunflower seed on the ground. "I didn't know there was going to be homework," he muttered.

Gary retrieved the postcard where Clara had written their to-do list. "Do you think the spell book is sealed up in someone else's basement? Someplace we could never find it?"

"I doubt it," said Clara. "Constance might not have known where it is, but…she seemed to think we could find it. It must be somewhere we can get to it."

"If that's true," Gary said, "it would have to be some-where that we can find, but that no one else would've found for 140 years. Otherwise, this is hopeless."

"What if somebody already found it?" Chris asked. "What if Constance wants us—or Clara, at least—to get it from the person who already figured out where it is?"

"I don't know how we'd find it then. If it's not in Biskop-skulla, it could be anywhere."

"You guys!" Chris exclaimed suddenly. "Whoever broke into Erik Mattsson's tomb was looking for *something*. What if it was one of the same things we're looking for?"

"The break-in was the same day that the bell fell on the bus, and Constance wrote about that specifically!" Clara interjected excitedly.

"Erik Mattsson died before Constance was born, but his tomb has been open to the public once a year for over a hundred years. Anyone could have hidden something small there, like a book, sometime along the way," Gary added.

"Oh gosh," Clara said, "If that's where it was hiding, I hope they got it out. I don't want to have to dig around in someone's coffin."

"I am *so* down to dig around in someone's coffin," Chris said.

"Yeah, that sounds awesome," Gary added.

Before they left for the day, they agreed that Gary would notify Chris and Clara as soon as the books they'd ordered arrived.

The next day, as she played badminton in PE, Clara wondered *why* someone would choose to violate Erik Mattsson's tomb. It was a pretty gutsy move, creating a distraction with the church bell and then opening the coffin when no one was looking. That wasn't a spur-of-the-moment decision; it was premeditated. Having no other evil villain at hand, Clara assumed it to be the work of Tad Trumpeter.

Did he have his own set of written instructions? Was he

working from clues left behind by someone else? Or did he have powers that helped him seek out the things he wished to find?

The last, she concluded, seemed unlikely to be the case. He'd been digging haphazardly in the earth next to the cemetery for more than a week now. If he had magic powers to direct him to a specific spot, he would have found whatever he was looking for by now.

He's searching, Clara thought, as she and her classmates headed into the locker room. *He only has a vague idea where to look. Like us.*

Clara was lost in her thoughts for most of the day. She could barely pay attention in English class, where most of class time was devoted to students taking turns reading the lines of the characters from *The Miracle Worker.* In pre-algebra she daydreamed about bones and books: hiding in walls, in basements, in attics, in furniture, in luggage. Their quest seemed so hopeless.

In American History they had a substitute teacher, who droned on for twenty minutes about the Reconstruction, then passed out some fill-in-the-blank worksheets.

Clara welcomed the opportunity to sit in silence. She filled in a handful of the blanks but had a hard time focusing on the worksheet.

The church, she thought. *I saw someone messing around in the steeple of the church.*

What if they had been looking for something too? What if the goal of that mysterious person—probably Tad—hadn't just been to unfasten the church bell? Her thoughts drifted absentmindedly. She wondered what a person could see from the church steeple. How far was it from the cemetery? How far was it from the school?

That's when it occurred to her to check the model of Biskopskulla that Mr. Froehlich kept under plexiglass in the back of the classroom.

Her desk was in the second-to-last row, so it wasn't difficult to steal a glance at the cluttered back half of the class-room. Three long tables held cardboard boxes and stacks of maps as well as the antique diorama.

It was huge, this model of the town: easily five feet by six feet. It occurred to Clara that most of the classrooms at Prairie Dale were used for storage as well as instruction, and that this was one difference between rural schools and urban schools. In a prairie state, where space is plentiful and students are few, a teacher could go for years without needing to declutter a room.

She scanned the buildings in the miniature town.

Then she stopped.

Each of the miniature houses was mounted on a block of wood. Presumably this was a convenient way to anchor the delicate replica structures onto the plywood frame on which the entire village was mounted. The "grass" of the model, which represented the lawns, much of the cemetery, and pretty much any land that wasn't paved, was represented by a patchwork of felt pieces carefully sewn together. The felt had probably once been bright green, but it had faded unevenly so that it was almost gray along two sides. The felt wasn't entirely flat, though—it had been applied on top of a thin layer of some type of padding, creating the impression that the landscape of the town rose and fell gently.

Near the facsimile of the village church, the felt grass rose up slightly, so that it obscured most of the wooden block to which both the church and the tomb of Erik Mattsson were affixed. Because the church was one of the largest buildings in the town, the wooden block was bigger than the blocks that supported the other buildings. It was about the size and shape of a hardback book. On the first day of class Clara would have noticed nothing unusual about this.

But today she saw that it looked like the wooden box in her basement. In fact, it looked *exactly* like the wooden box in her basement, down to the gentle carvings on the side.

"Clara Hutchins?" the substitute teacher said loudly, reading the name off the attendance chart. "Are you having a problem?"

Clara snapped to attention. "Sorry!" she said. "I was looking for the pencil sharpener." The teacher looked skeptical. "I'm new," Clara added, which drew a nod of understanding.

It had been months, of course, since Clara started school. But the other students only looked up momentarily from their own desks. A couple of them pointed to the pencil sharpener, plainly visible in the front of the classroom. To them, she was the new kid. She had a sneaking suspicion that she'd be the new kid right up through graduation day.

As Clara walked up to sharpen her perfectly sharp pencil, she couldn't wait to tell Gary and Chris what she'd discovered.

Later that night, still grounded, Clara called Chris's house first, because she knew he was less likely than Gary to be sitting down to a family dinner. The phone rang and rang, but no one answered, and it didn't go to voice mail. She wished he had a cell phone. Next she called Gary and explained what she suspected—that there was a wooden puzzle box hidden in the town diorama, perhaps with the missing book inside.

"That makes sense," Gary said. "What if someone had been told to look for the book in the church, or under the tomb, or whatever, and they didn't realize they were supposed to look in the diorama, not the real tomb? I mean, it could even have been one of Constance's prophecies. She's not always a hundred percent clear about what she's seeing." He sounded more impressed with himself for understanding this about the box than with Clara for discovering its whereabouts.

"Now we just have to…break into the school or something," Clara said.

Gary cleared his throat. "I think I have an idea."

23

At the next scholastic bowl practice, Gary barely buzzed in at all, and when he did, he answered the questions incorrectly.

"Gary!" Mrs. Maynard said gently, after he'd confused the battles of Antietam and Appomattox. "I thought you knew that one."

"Sorry, Mrs. Maynard," he said. "I just wasn't thinking."

At the end of practice Mrs. Maynard announced the team's line-up for the district preliminaries that Saturday. The "starting team," the players who would be seated at the beginning of each round of competition, would be Clara, Gary, Myron, Edison, and Kaitlyn. In the second half of each game, Chris would replace Gary.

"No hard feelings, buddy," Chris said. "I know I'm new at this."

"None taken!" Gary said—this was, after all, exactly the outcome he'd been counting on. "This way, everyone gets to play."

"That's sportsmanship!" said Mrs. Maynard. "Or sports-womanship. But in this case, sportsmanship."

After practice, Clara was eager to share what she'd learned from her self-assigned homework. Just days earlier, Gary had received the new Olle Gardell books. She stayed up very late that night, reading in her room. She stopped when the words started to blur. Ordinarily, she considered reading assignments to be the lowest-priority homework imaginable—why waste time reading a textbook when you could just skim it and figure out the most important stuff? But this time, she read as if her life depended on it. Because it just might.

The air was chilly, but she and Chris and Gary chose to sit outside on the grass, jackets zipped tightly, their hands in their pockets.

Gary started by explaining what he'd gleaned from Gardell's Iceland book.

"He wrote a little about the overall nature of witchcraft. It's like he's spelling it out for kids. So witchcraft is all about *enchantment*," he began. "And enchantment is like...cooking."

"An enchantment is like a spell, right?" Clara asked.

"I mean, basically. But think of a spell like a recipe, okay? The ingredients could be physical things, like a bone, or a special kind of water, or a flower. But the ingredients for an enchantment can *also* be words, special words, that must be spoken in a particular order. Or the ingredients could be something intangible, like a thought, or a wish. Or a place or a time."

"And then there's the subject of an enchantment," Gary continued. "Like, the object you're enchanting. A dowsing rod, for example. You find a stick that's the right shape, and you implement the spell—"

"Meaning, you follow the recipe?" Clara interjected.

"Right, yeah. You follow the recipe of the spell, whatever spell makes a dowsing rod, and then when you're done, that object has a magical property."

Chris nodded, as if this were a perfectly normal discussion to be having. "How long does it last?"

"Depends on the spell. Some of them expire after a certain amount of time, and some of them last forever. And enchantments have a natural psychological camouflage. They're not impossible to see, and they don't erase your memory, but they bend reality in a way that makes you doubt yourself. It's just a natural consequence of magic. The funny thing is, a lot of sources say that the aversion to magic increases as you get older. So, little kids have an easier time than adults noticing if something is enchanted."

Clara had read a book by Olle Gardell about the witches of Ecuador.

"What I found out," Clara said, "was that really strong magic—say, something that lasts forever—is harder to do. Like, the ingredients are rare, or the words you have to say are trickier."

"The *incantation*," Chris said. "If you have more people saying the incantation, that can make it stronger too."

"I didn't know that," Gary said. "That's good to know. The other thing I found is that sometimes magical objects just seem to occur naturally, but most of the time they have to be made. It's kinda like some stones can be naturally magnetic, but then you can also take a non-magnetic piece of metal and magnetize it."

"So something like the philosopher's stone, right?" Chris said. "Is that naturally occurring? Or would you have to make that? That was supposedly a rock that could turn metals into gold," he told Clara.

"I knew that!" she replied.

"I don't know," Gary said with a shrug. "Olle Gardell doesn't seem to think the philosopher's stone ever existed. But some people think a witch made one in the Middle Ages, and he showed it off, and then medieval scientists spent a long time—like, *centuries*—trying to figure out how to make another one like it."

"I don't think they did, though. I mean, if they had figured out how to turn lead into gold, then I really don't think gold would still be valuable today," said Clara.

"Or maybe they did, but it only lasted for twenty minutes and there wasn't that much lead around. Or maybe they made a philosopher's stone, but it could turn only one ounce of lead into gold per year. If the enchantment wasn't very strong. Maybe they couldn't find enough dragon blood, or whatever, to make a stronger spell."

"I...don't think dragons are real," Clara said.

Chris looked at her blankly. "I'm not willing to commit to that."

"Anyway…what I read," Clara said, "is that magic in people is like magic in objects. As in, some people are just kind of naturally magical, and some people become enchanted because they follow a recipe. The book I read compared it to being musical. Some people have perfect pitch, and they just naturally can learn the name of a musical note and then they can identify that same note any time they hear it—"

"Or you can ask them to sing a D-sharp and they can just automatically sing D-sharp," Gary interrupted.

"Yeah, like that. You can just be born with that ability. But if you never try to sing or play music, you might have perfect pitch and not ever know that you have it. So, there might be people who are born, and live their whole lives, and die, without ever knowing that they are magical."

"That's pretty sad," Chris said.

"Everything is pretty sad, eventually," Gary said.

"Truth."

"So, what do you guys think? Was Constance naturally gifted, or did she learn magic?" Gary asked.

"Well, that's the thing," said Clara. "We only know that she had one magical ability: seeing the future."

"Actually," said Gary, "if she only had that one magical ability, then we wouldn't be getting ingredients for a spell that she put together for us."

"Valid point," said Clara.

"She was a seer, I think," said Chris. "Some seers can see the future, some of them can see the past, and some seers can tell what people are thinking. But they can be the most powerful witches, because they can figure things out without having to study them. Constance could have been some kind of super-witch if she hadn't bit it."

"Hey!" Gary said, "you're talking about one of Clara's relatives, watch how you speak."

"Sorry. If she hadn't *bought* it."

Mrs. Mahler pulled up in a blue station wagon.

"Good job, guys," Gary said. "Keep doing your home-work."

On Saturday morning, the kids arrived at the school an hour before the first match of the scholastic bowl to help Mrs. Maynard prepare the school. Several parents had volunteered to be officians, including Mrs. Mahler, who had decided at the last minute against wearing a Prairie Dale Middle School sweatshirt. "Might make me seem biased!" she said with a wink.

Kaitlyn showed up at the library fifteen minutes late, her stepmother in tow. "I am so sorry!" she said. "We are honestly both so *contrite*."

Gary whispered to Chris, "Five bucks says she was late on purpose just so she could say that." Chris smirked.

Preparing the school for a scholastic bowl meet was a simple process. The library was the tournament headquarters, but because absolutely no food or drinks were allowed, the teachers' lounge was designated as a special room for the coaches and moderators. During the tournament no students would be allowed inside, but this morning Clara and Kaitlyn were tasked with making coffee and cutting prepackaged muffins in half before arranging them on plates.

The rest of the team unlocked the classrooms to be used for the competition and rearranged the furniture so there would be two tables in the front of each room for the two opposing teams in each match, plus a podium facing the teams for the moderator.

Because he was the strongest member of the team, Gary was tasked with hauling boxes of supplies from the supply closet to the library. The supplies included extra coffee, paper towels, cleaning materials, and trophies and medals that would be awarded at the end of the day.

Being in charge of the supply closet for the day meant that Gary was also in charge of the *key* to the supply closet. Mrs. Maynard was the tournament director, and the tournament regulations required her to be available to communicate with coaches in the event of an emergency or a dispute about the rules.

"Make sure you don't lose that, Mr. Mahler," Mrs. Maynard told him when she entrusted the key to his care at seven-thirty that morning. "And don't forget that at about two, I'll need you to start moving the medals into the cafeteria for the awards assembly."

"Will do, Mrs. M."

What Gary knew, and what Mrs. Maynard didn't know he knew, was that the key to the supply closet was identical to the master key for the middle school. Whether this was a coincidence or by design Gary had no idea. He had learned this secret from Seth Van Oosten the previous year. Seth was the team captain and an A student. He felt it was his sacred duty to pass on the wisdom about the supply-closet key to a younger member of the team, just as it had been passed down to him from an upperclassman. Together Gary and Seth sneaked a peek inside the girls' locker room after hours. There were no girls present, of course, but they both observed that it was much cleaner and didn't smell as bad as the boys' locker room.

This time Gary was focused on the one classroom door he wanted to unlock: Mr. Froehlich's history classroom, with its antique model of Biskopskulla sprawling across a table in the back.

He had rehearsed the heist carefully with Clara and Chris the night before. Fortunately, it was a cold day, and the school's heating system was always set low on weekends to conserve energy, so Gary could get away with wearing a denim jacket indoors. He needed some tools, and his jacket had pockets that were big enough to hold supplies and still snap shut.

He patted the pocket containing a Phillips-head screw-driver and then willed himself to stop thinking about it as the first of the opposing teams showed up at the main entrance to the school. First things first: there was a tournament to try to win.

The tournament involved six local schools. They would face off in pairs until every team had competed once against every other team, which meant there would be five matches throughout the day. The meet didn't attract much of an audience. A few parents showed up, along with the other teams, as well as a couple of younger siblings. Kaitlyn's stepmother and Mrs. Mahler were volunteering to help out all day, as was Edison's American host: a retired postal worker named Ellen.

Because of her schedule Clara's mother would be sleeping for the first few hours of the day, but she had promised to pick up Myron's mother, who was volunteering on the other side of town, so that the two women could catch the last two hours of the tournament later in the afternoon.

The first match of the day pitted Prairie Dale Middle School against Gävle Middle School. Unlike most of the schools in the region, the Gävle students had matching team sweatshirts that read "GMS Scholastic Bowl," and on the back was printed "Born To Buzz!"

The students of both teams settled into their seats as the moderator, a coach from one of the other schools, took the podium and welcomed everyone. Once it was time to start, she placed a digital stopwatch on the podium in front of her.

"Our first toss-up question!" she read. "Survivors of the Cocoanut Grove fire in Boston were the first burn victims to be successfully treated with this medicine…" She paused briefly. "…which was famously discovered by accident… after a Petri dish became contaminated with mold." She was trying very hard to speak slowly and clearly. "For ten points—"

A member of the Gävle team activated their buzzer.

The moderator recognized the dark-haired girl who had buzzed in. "Carla?"

"Calamine?" said Carla.

"Incorrect," said the moderator. She continued the question. "Name this group of antibiotics first isolated by Alexander Fleming."

Gary hit his buzzer.

"Gary," said the moderator.

"Penicillin?" Gary said.

"Correct! Your team gets the bonus question." This meant the Prairie Dale students had the chance to answer a three-part question, and to talk to each other while answering it.

"At the age of twenty-five," the moderator began, "this man earned the wrath of William Randolph Hearst, America's wealthiest newspaper publisher, by basing a movie on his life. For ten points each: Name the man who wrote, directed, and starred in *Citizen Kane.*"

"I know this!" said Kaitlyn, who was serving as team captain this round. "Orson Welles."

"Correct," said the moderator. "Before he was a filmmaker, Orson Welles helped cause a panic when he directed a radio broadcast based on what classic science fiction novel?"

"I know this, it's *War of the Worlds*," said Edison softly. Myron nodded in agreement, so Kaitlyn let Edison answer.

"Correct!" There was one more part to the question. "William Randolph Hearst famously hired Richard Outcault, the creator of the first color comic strip. What was the name of that comic strip?"

Kaitlyn threw her hands up and then gestured to her teammates. "Anybody?"

"I think….maybe?" Gary said, and Kaitlyn gave him a thumbs-up. "The Yellow Kid?"

"Can you be more specific?" said the moderator.

"No. No I cannot."

"I'm sorry, that's not enough. The name of the comic

strip was *Hogan's Alley*. The Yellow Kid was a character in it."

Gary nodded sagely. He hadn't scored a point, but looking across the table, they could see that the other team seemed intimidated.

By the end of the match, Prairie Dale was ahead by thirty-five points. Clara had answered two questions—including one about *Wuthering Heights*—and the entire team was in high spirits. Gävle Middle School's squad usually presented a significant threat, and beating them boded well for the rest of the tournament.

Prairie Dale won against their next opponent, a team whose captain was having an allergy attack so severe that his sneezing forced Mrs. Maynard to pause the game, and the next, against a team whose members were all sixth graders.

After lunch, it was time for Gary to implement his plan. As he had for the morning's matches, Gary played only the first half of the game.

Once the moderator's stopwatch signaled that it was halftime, Gary stood up and Chris took his spot. Gary gave a thumbs-up to his team as he excused himself to help set up the library. He was getting started a few minutes early, but who would complain about that?

The hallway was empty except for a grade-school kid from Kewanee who had come to watch his two brothers compete. Gary pointed him toward the bathrooms and continued down the hall and around the corner, to Mr. Froehlich's classroom.

Gary stopped outside the door. He could feel sweat on his palms. He looked around to see if anyone else was in the hallway. He didn't know exactly what the consequences would be if he was caught breaking into a classroom, but they couldn't be good. He might get suspended. He would definitely have some explaining to do, and right now that was the last thing he needed.

Glancing around again, he tried the key in the lock. It turned and he opened the door and slipped into the room.

When he tried to pull the key back out of the lock, it wouldn't budge.

Oh no, thought Gary. It would be impossible to pretend he hadn't been up to mischief if the key got stuck in the door. He wiggled the key and tried pulling it out two more times. No luck. As a last resort, he pushed the key in and then yanked hard. It slid out of the lock so quickly he almost lost his balance.

Gary shut the door behind him—an open door would surely be a red flag to anyone who happened to walk by. He didn't turn the lights on. The windows along the classroom wall provided sufficient light to find his way to the back of the room.

Gary took the screwdriver out of his jacket pocket and began removing the screws that held the plexiglass lid in place over the model of Biskopskulla. He placed all six of the screws into his pants pocket so he wouldn't lose them.

The flat lid rested on clear plexiglass walls. It hadn't occurred to him to worry about how heavy it might be, but it was big—almost too large for him to reach from one end to the other with his arms fully extended. He gripped the lid as well as he could with his fingertips and pulled up, first gently, and then with increasing force. For a moment, it seemed immovable (was it glued down?), but then the seal formed by years of contact broke, and the lid came up in his hands.

Fortunately, the village church was close enough to the edge of the model that he didn't have to completely remove the lid. He merely slid it aside far enough to give him access to the church and the suspiciously shaped wood block underneath. For a moment he wondered who'd made this replica in the first place. Mr. Froehlich had never seemed to know.

Gary lifted the church up. It was attached with craft glue

and poster nails and was covered in a fine layer of dust. He set the model church down next to the case and focused his attention on the wooden box upon which it had rested for decades.

As far as he could tell, it was identical to the box that Clara had discovered in her basement. Years of exposure to light had faded the varnish on the very edges of the box, but the rectangular patch on the top which had—until recently—been covered by the miniature church remained as dark as the wooded exterior of the box from the basement.

Gary held the box to his ear and shook it. He wasn't sure, but he thought he could hear movement. If there was a book inside, he could worry later about how to get it out.

Gary took a solid wooden block out of his jacket pocket. Chris had found an excuse to create it in shop class, out of a castoff from another project. It was exactly the same size and shape as the book boxes, and had been stained the same color, more or less.

He stuck the old box into his denim jacket and directed his attention to putting the model back together. He felt like Indiana Jones, replacing the wooden box with a rough replica, and then smoothing the green felt around it to look natural.

His plan was just to set the model church onto the block and call it a day, but a few beads of dried glue on the bottom of the church made it sit precariously askew. No problem; he took a piece of gum from his pocket, chewed it furiously for ten seconds, then used it to fasten the church firmly in place.

He glanced up at the classroom clock. He had only been here a few minutes, but it felt like a dangerously long time. He stretched his fingers and repositioned the plexiglass, then quickly screwed the first two screws back in. The third one got stuck halfway in, and it took a few seconds for him to screw it back out and straighten it while his hands shook nervously.

Finally, his job was done.

He straightened his jacket and turned toward the door.

A large black bird stood on a desk near the door, watching him. It was a raven, about two feet long, and its eyes were large and intelligent. Gary jumped back, and when the bird flapped its wings and flew toward him, he fell backward, knocking over several desks with a clatter. Gary could hear footsteps hurrying down the hallway toward the room.

So much for avoiding discovery.

The first person through the door was a custodian, Mrs. Beeth, who always seemed to despise middle-school students. She was followed by Mrs. Maynard, and then…his mother? A few coaches from other teams must have been free as well, and they crowded around the classroom door.

Gary stood up.

"Gary," Mrs. Maynard began. "It looks like you were horsing around in here when you should have been working. What are you doing in Mr. Froelich's room?"

Mrs. Mahler looked absolutely aghast, but she said nothing.

Gary couldn't think of a decent lie to tell, so he told a truth.

"There was a bird—" he began.

"A bird?" said Mrs. Maynard.

"Like a crow. No—a raven, I think. I saw it in here and I thought I should try to…let it out. It was crazy big, for a bird." He realized too late that the last detail probably made it sound like he was making this up.

"So you saw a bird and you didn't think to tell anyone?"

"I didn't think it would be so hard to get a bird to go out a window!" he said sheepishly. "I'm so sorry."

"Sounds like a fib, buster," said Mrs. Beeth in a deep voice. "I make sure the doors and windows are locked every Friday, and I've never seen a raven inside this school. You're getting a week of detention, at least."

Just then a coach from Cambridge Middle School said, "Well, would you look at that?" He picked something up off the floor from in front of the teacher's desk.

"I don't know what else that could come from but an Illinois common raven," he said, holding up a shiny black feather. "Funny thing is, they're not all that common this time of year." He looked up at the classroom windows. "There's your problem. The seal on this window expanded and the latch didn't close. It's not your fault," he said to the custodian. "Same thing happened to me at my summer cabin last year. It's the weather."

"Gary," Mrs. Maynard said. "You should have come and got me."

"Yeah, I was pretty stupid," Gary agreed, repositioning the desks and straightening his jacket. He patted the pocket which contained the box.

Mission accomplished.

Gary rejoined his team for the final match of the day. He gave a small smile and a secret thumbs up to Clara and Chris to let them know his task was completed. Prairie Dale had fared surprisingly well, having lost only one match so far—to the squad from Genesee Junior High School, a much larger school.

"Do you know what the Genesee mascot is?" Gary confided after the loss. "The Genesee Rabbits. Stupid, stupid rabbits, always bringing bad luck."

Myron in particular was having a stellar day, because each round contained both history and sports questions, which were his specialty. He'd answered an average of four toss-up questions per game.

The only other school with a comparable record, Woodall, was scheduled to face Prairie Dale for the last round. This meant that Prairie Dale, for the first time in years, was in a position to qualify for the sectional championship tournament. The top two schools from today would advance.

"Pressure's on," said Gary, as he settled into the seat previously occupied by Chris, between Myron and Clara. He was eager to put the stress of the early afternoon behind him.

"Thank you for reminding us, Gary, but the answers are the same whether we feel pressure or not, so we might as well stay calm," Myron said flatly.

"Indeed," said Gary.

The match began well for Woodall, who answered a math toss-up and a chemistry toss-up, as well as several bonus questions. Then Edison buzzed in on a question about Egyptian mythology but got the answer wrong. Clara could tell by the way Chris squirmed in the audience that he'd known the answer.

On the next question, Prairie Dale's fortunes began to shift. "This planet makes a complete orbit around the sun in about 4,333 Earth days," the moderator began. "It has an atmosphere made up mostly of hydrogen and helium. This planet's Great Red Spot is—"

Boom! Gary banged his buzzer just a split-second before a girl on the Woodall team.

"Gary?"

"Jupiter!"

"That's correct."

Although Prairie Dale only got one of the bonus questions correct, Gary's excitement energized his team.

Woodall's math whiz struck again at the beginning of the second half, but then Chris buzzed in on a question about spark-ignition engines ("I live at a junkyard," he explained) and Prairie Dale was back in the running.

Clara attempted to buzz in twice during the second half, but she was a moment too late both times. She tried to concentrate only on the voice of the moderator, but the last two questions were virtually impossible; no one buzzed in.

An egg-shaped timer beeped on top of the moderator's podium.

"That is time," she said. "But we have an unusual situation. The teams are tied, which means that three toss-up questions will be read during an overtime."

The first question was about Australian history, and neither team felt confident enough to answer. The second overtime question was a fairly obscure question about organic chemistry. Edison's hand hovered over his buzzer, but he didn't want to risk getting it wrong and getting the rest of his team shut out.

That meant that the final overtime toss-up question would be sudden death: if either team got it right, they would win the entire match.

The moderator cleared her throat. "In 1949, he achieved the triple crown of American theater, winning the Pulitzer Prize, the New York Drama Critics Circle Award, and the Tony. His play *The Crucible*—"

Clara slammed the button down on her buzzer.

"Clara?"

"Arthur Miller."

"That's correct."

Kaitlyn let out a squeak. It was over. The Prairie Dale team would take second in today's tournament, and that meant they had qualified to advance to the sectional tournament.

The team went through the polite formality of thanking the other team for a good match before getting hard slaps on the back from Edison. Kaitlyn was almost too excited to talk. Even Myron and Chris gave each other a fist bump.

Clara suddenly wondered where Gary was. *I need to share this with my best friend,* she thought, and then realized: She had never had a guy for a best friend before, but it was true. She felt comfortable with the other kids on the team, and she was actually starting to adore Chris as if he were a little brother, but she knew she couldn't fully process a major development like this until she shared it with Gary.

He had been in the back of the room for most of the second half of the match, but he must have slipped out before the match went into overtime.

Mrs. Maynard had heard the good news, because she materialized at the classroom door, beaming. As the team made their way toward the library, Clara's mom and Mrs. Mahler caught up and congratulated them.

Gary was waiting in the library, clearing off tables. Clara tried to figure out if he had heard, but when he walked up and hugged her, she assumed he had.

"We have to talk," he said in a low voice. He made eye contact with Chris, and the three of them convened next to the bookshelves.

"You guys remember Raymond Bergstrom?" Gary asked.

"He's the guy who flipped out at the Eatery, isn't he?" Clara said.

"That's him."

"What happened?"

"He was murdered."

24

Holy carp," Chris said, with a whistle. "What was it he said? 'They're after me.' Sounds like he was right."

"That's terrible," Clara said.

"Yeah, almost as bad as the next thing he said," Gary added. "Remember? 'If they get me, they'll get you.'"

"We can't die," said Chris. "We have sectionals in a few weeks."

"Also, the rest of our *lives* to live," Clara pointed out. "How...how did he die?"

"He fell out a third-story window in the old Biskopskulla dormitory building," Gary said. "Landed head first in a barrel of artisanal soap." Then, when Clara looked puzzled, he added, "The Vintage Goods Gift Shop is on the first floor of the dorm building. They had some stuff out on display."

"How do you know about this already?" asked Clara.

"I was in the hallway. Gossip in a small town travels at the speed of sound."

"Are the cops really sure it's murder?" asked Chris.

"No, they think it's an accident. But *I'm* pretty sure. Aren't you?"

25

The three of them convened in Clara's basement room the next night while her mom tried out a recipe for zucchini bread upstairs. Gary brought the new box, still unopened. Chris brought a rock newly chipped off the Häxa Stone and some homemade beef jerky, which Clara decided not to taste.

There was definitely something inside the diorama's box, but whatever mechanism served to open this new box, it was different from the one from Clara's basement wall. In just about every other way, the boxes were identical—the same size, the same weight, the same type of wood. This box, however, was sealed shut and would not open no matter how many times they spun it.

"I'm telling you," Chris said. "A coping saw. I can get one from home; it'll take off the edge of the box neat and clean. It's made for detail work."

The other two weren't sure. It felt wrong to damage the box if there was some other way to open it. The Häxa Stone glowed brightly next to the box, but there was no way to know whether the box, its contents, or both were enchanted. Frustrated, they sat in a circle on the green shag carpet, the box on the ground before them.

"What should we do?" asked Clara. "We have to see what's inside, and we don't have much time!"

Forty minutes later, Chris returned to the basement with his coping saw. It had one handle and a sharp, narrow blade stretched across a U-shaped frame, almost like a violin's bow.

Clara winced when Chris began sawing into the end of the antique box, but in no time he had neatly separated the wooden panel at the end. He tilted the box to one side. At first, nothing came out. Then Chris gave the box a good shake and a leather-bound book slid into his hands. Its cover was plain and black, and it looked to be much better preserved than Clara's book. "Book two," Gary said.

Chris flipped through the book. "There's not a lot of writing. Doesn't look full."

They opened it and started to read. The tenth page contained a note.

Dear Girl,

I see you more clearly now. There is another in your company, and yet a third I can scarcely glimpse. That's the way it often is—some futures clear as day, some futures dim as a foggy night. Make certain you trust your confidants, and follow the instructions herein.

Time is short; I have seen my own end. Would that I Could help you to avoid yours.

The note was signed *C. Love*. The next page was labeled *the Spell of Protection*, and it listed a set of conditions and instructions. These included

Time: When the longest night begins

Place: Upon the Altar at the Sepulchre; where the Disappearing Girl of Biskopskulla was last seen

Elements: The Blood of my Blood, The Bones of my Body, The Words of the Spell, consumed by Flames.

"Blood. Bones. Words," Gary said. "Great. Where are they?" The next page was labeled *The Words of the Spell*. The "words" were unintelligible. The page was covered in what appeared to be writing, but even the letters were unrecognizable. "Ugh. Do we have to figure out what language this is?"

"Maybe not," Chris said. "Maybe we just burn it. 'The words of the spell, consumed by flames'—maybe fire activates them?"

"That seems to be what she's telling us," Clara agreed.

The next page had no heading, but it contained a vertical line with boxes drawn at irregular intervals along it. One of the boxes, at the top of the line, had a circle in the center and a star along one side. The box at the bottom had three tiny figures in a circle with their heads pointing toward the center.

"What *is* this?" Clara said to no one in particular.

"Looks like a Christmas decoration," Chris said. "Or maybe a fishing line."

"Great," Clara said. "A fishing line. What else does she tell us?"

Gary turned to the next page, which was blank, as was the next, and the next.

"Is that it?" asked Chris. "Is the rest empty? Seems like a waste to use a whole book. She could have fit that in a letter."

Gary flipped through every page until he got to the last one. "Here's something."

There was text on the very last page of the book.

It read, *That I do not know, for those I cannot see. But you must find them, or the spell will be for naught.*

"Huh," said Gary. "That's a weird epilogue."

"Here," said Clara. She uncapped a pen, took the book from him, turned back one page, and wrote: *Where can we find the bones?*

"I was thinking of doing that while you were leafing through the pages," she told Gary. "I'm sure that's the question she was answering."

"Whoa," said Chris, "She answered your question before you wrote it."

"She answered that question a hundred and forty years ago," Clara pointed out.

"True, but I didn't know it could work like that. That's crazy."

"What about the Disappearing Girl of Biskopskulla?" Clara asked. "You guys are from here. Have you ever heard of that?" Both boys admitted that they hadn't, but Gary pledged to look into it.

By the end of the night, Clara was feeling almost optimistic, until Gary reminded her on his way out the door, "Now we're out of clues."

26

At nine o'clock the next night, Gary called Clara. "I found an unsolved mystery that matches the profile of what we're looking for," Gary began. His phone calls seldom involved much small talk.

He told Clara about a girl who had gone missing almost thirty years earlier.

"Her family was baffled, cops were baffled; they never found her."

"The disappearing girl," Clara began. "What was it? *Where the Disappearing Girl of Biskopskulla...was last seen?*"

"It was a big deal at the time. Now nobody really mentions her." He read a snippet of the second news article he'd found. "Jennifer Fahren was last seen at her home on 1900th Street in Gävle, Illinois—"

"Nineteen-*hundredth* Street," Clara began. "Gosh, that's the middle of nowhere. But—Gävle? I thought we wanted someone who'd disappeared from Biskopskulla?"

"That's the crazy thing!" Gary said. "I looked up her family's old house on the map. It's in Gävle now, but it's in the northwest part of town. It's a place that—before Gävle was settled—used to be part of Biskopskulla. At least, part of the original Biskopskulla colony."

"Ooh," Clara said. "I don't know why, but that makes it seem even more significant."

Gary was silent.

"Hello, Gary?"

"Clara..." Gary said, his voice low and serious. "I think there's someone outside my window."

"Yikes, that's creepy," Clara said instinctively. "Are you sure?"

"Clara, I live on the second floor. I think someone climbed up on my roof. I'm gonna turn my lights off and see if I can see them better. Okay," he said softly, "pretending not to look, pretending not to look, one, two, three—"

Clara heard a terrified shout, and then heard Gary yelling, "Who are you—?"

And then the phone went silent.

"Gary?" Clara said, but the call disconnected. She called him again, but there was no answer. She called again, and it went straight to voicemail. Clara felt sick. What if Gary was in some sort of trouble? On the other hand, what if he was just overreacting?

For a moment, she froze. Then she dialed 911.

She struggled to explain to the operator why she was calling. "I was just on the phone with my friend, and he—the call—hung up suddenly. I am worried that he might be in danger."

"Do you know his address?" the dispatcher asked.

"Not off the top of my head," Clara said, scrambling to see if Gary's street address was written down somewhere in her room. "It's on Flower Street," she said. Then, remembering the size of the town, she added, "It's the Mahlers. Gary Mahler and his parents."

"Oh!" said the dispatcher. "Yes, we know where the Mahlers live. Yes; an officer is on the way. I have a few more questions for you."

As Clara gave as much information as she could, she felt increasingly guilty. What if this was all unnecessary? Or, what if Gary was just joking with her? *If that's the case*, she thought, *this will teach him there are some things you don't joke about.*

A few minutes later, after she'd gotten off the phone with 911, she tried Gary's number again.

There was still no response.

There was nothing to do but wait.

Clara poured herself a glass of water and felt worry turn

to panic. Gary was a middle-school kid all alone in his parents' big house tonight. Just like her.

She checked the front door and the back door to make sure they were locked. She thought about what Gary had said—"I think there's someone outside my window"—and closed all of the drapes on the first floor of the house. She didn't want to go upstairs, or down to the basement, because she figured the first floor had the most escape routes. She tried calling Chris, but he seldom answered unless he was expecting a call.

She turned on all the lights on the first floor. Every sound she heard, all the routine creaks and groans of an old house at night, made her jump. She thought about turning on the TV as a distraction but rejected the idea because then she might not hear if someone approached. She tried to read a novel, but she found it impossible to focus.

After an hour of waiting, her phone rang. It was Gary.

"What happened?"

"Uh, there was definitely someone outside the window. I couldn't tell who it was, but when I turned out the light to get a better look, we were looking right at each other."

"Was it Tad?"

"I don't think so. The person seemed skinnier. But there's something else. It looked like the person was floating twenty feet up in the air. And then suddenly they weren't there."

"I called 911."

"I know, the police got here pretty quick, actually."

"What did you tell them?"

"Well, I didn't tell them I saw someone floating. I just said that I saw a trespasser outside the window and I tried to describe them, but it was too sudden and too dark. And then they searched the property."

"Did they find anything?"

"Yeah. There was a coat. Up in the tree next to the house, maybe eighteen feet up. An old military surplus coat, wrapped around a big branch. It was like someone had put it there to make a more comfortable place to sit."

"Did the police keep the coat?"

"Yeah, I guess they did," Gary said. "I got the impression they think it's some kind of prank."

"Maybe—" Clara said, hopefully, "Maybe it *was* just a prank, maybe by someone at school?"

"You didn't see what happened," Gary said. "Someone was watching me, Clara."

"If that's the case, why you? I mean, let's say it's not Tad, but maybe it's an associate of his. A minion, something like that. Why are *you* the one they're spying on?"

"Why would we assume I'm the only one?"

They talked some more, but it was this question that haunted Clara after she hung up the phone. She forced herself to open the drapes and peer out into the night air. A thin layer of autumn fog had descended over Biskopskulla, turning the houses in the distance into dark shadows flecked with golden spots where windows glowed.

She stayed awake until her mother came home.

27

It wasn't difficult to find an excuse to go to the Gävle Public Library. Gary, Chris, and Clara got a ride there the following morning from Gary's dad. The archives of the *Gävle-Woodhill Review*, the only truly local newspaper covering the Biskopskulla region, went back only three years on the newspaper's website. Older issues of the *Review* were archived at the Gävle Public Library, and quite possibly nowhere else in the world.

Clara stationed herself at one of two ancient computers located on the first floor of the library. The screen featured glowing green letters on a black background. She'd never seen anything like it. It reminded her of the way old movies depicted the future: spaceships that could go faster than light but had consoles with computer graphics from the 1970s.

Clara's task was to find any original, unpublished documents in the library archives that pertained to Constance Love or her family. Because this was not just the official library of the city of Gävle but served the entire township, it was the repository for certain historic artifacts that were not in the county museum.

Chris looked through a bound directory of the archives of the *Gävle-Woodhill Review*. Because the directory was not digitized, he couldn't conduct a keyword search. Instead, he used one of the tiny pencils nearby to fill out a records request. The back issues of the newspaper were stored on microfiche, flat squares of film containing photographs of each page of the newspaper. These were kept behind the Circulation & Reference Desk.

After filling out his request, Chris stood at the desk and rang the bell. The back-room door opened, and a very tall, thin woman with gray hair pulled into a tight bun emerged and approached the desk.

"Good morning! What can I do for you, young lady?" she asked.

"Uh, I just need some old newspapers. On microfiche," he said, in a voice as deep as he could muster.

"I'm so sorry, young man. Let me look those up for you!"

"That's okay. It's a long-hair thing, I guess," Chris said with a shrug.

The newspaper back issues Chris requested covered August and September 1981. Chris and Gary positioned delicate squares of film onto the microfiche reader and examined the enlarged images of each page, scanning for any information about Jennifer Fahren. Fortunately, the *Gävle-Woodhill Review* published weekly rather than daily, and the issues were seldom more than ten pages long.

Gary skimmed through articles about athletic tournaments at the various local schools, or about small family restaurants changing owners. He was amused to see that one of his teachers, the portly Mr. Simons, had finished first place in the 1981 Hawley Douglas Crazy Bomber 5K.

"Whoa. Dime me!" Chris barked as he refocused the microfiche reader.

Gary handed him a dime, which Chris used to make a printout of the article he'd been reading. Then Chris zoomed in on the photographs accompanying the article and inserted another dime to print the enlarged images.

"Look at that!" Gary exclaimed, reading the printout. "Clara, come look at this!" he yelled, earning a stern look and a "sshhhh!" from the librarian.

"Oh my gosh," Clara said, reading over his shoulder.

The article was just one paragraph long. It explained that Jennifer "Jenny" Fahren, a high school student, age fifteen, had been missing for ten days; her mother missed her very much, and if anyone had information about her whereabouts, or the whereabouts of an adult man with whom she'd been seen, they should please contact the Gävle Police Department. The article did not mention where Jenny had last been seen. The first photograph was a black-and-white school picture of Jenny Fahren, a plain girl with dark hair and sad eyes. The other picture was captioned, "Theodore Herald. Photo credit Brandy Fredericks." It showed a man outdoors, wearing a work shirt and carrying a garden rake in his gloved right hand. He was in the process of raising his other hand as if to gesture, *Don't take my picture.*

Even in black and white, his identity was unmistakable. Except for a small mustache, the man in the photograph looked exactly like Tad Trumpeter. But he didn't look thirty years younger; he didn't even look a day younger. It was impossible, but to Clara, Chris, and Gary it was clear: Theodore Herald had come back to town, after nearly three decades, and he hadn't aged a day.

Just how old *was* he?

28

The rumors about Constance Love began to vex her sister Mary. None of the townsfolk would gossip about Constance *directly* when they talked to Mary, of course. But she could overhear them in the general store when she was buying flour, or gossiping in the market as she passed by.

"I heard someone say—it's simply preposterous, mind you—that Mr. Kronberg, the farmer, said a cruel word to Constance in the town square and the next day his crops had withered and died."

Or, "There's even talk—I don't believe it for an instant, of course—that Mrs. Carlson refused to extend credit to Constance at the general store. Constance whispered something to her for a good solid minute—this is what I've heard said—and that night, poor Mrs. Carlson birthed a child with no head!"

The most dark and salacious rumors were never told in the presence of Mary Love Olofsson—for she was the sweeter sister.

"A family from Altona was traveling through and their youngest girl went missing. I fear witchcraft is the purpose—"

"It was Constance, don't you know—"

"Constance killed her!—"

"Constance *ate her*!—"

At first, Mary pooh-poohed any notion that the whispers about her younger sister might represent a danger. But one day, Carl Olofsson, her husband, came home from the mill white as a sheet.

"It's more than just words, Mary," he said. "They mean to do her harm."

The two of them agreed that Constance should take leave of the colony, at least for a little while.

"Just until everyone calms down," Carl said, and Mary nodded, trying not to cry.

Carl counted out a small bit of money he'd been saving and the two of them went together to Constance's room, to explain what they'd decided.

They found her waiting for them, her bags already packed.

29

Clara woke up early and made herself an English muffin with cream cheese. She decided to pack an extra one for Chris, because she felt pretty sure he didn't eat very well at home, and then she decided she'd better make one for Gary, too, so that Chris wouldn't feel singled out.

She set out walking to Gary's house, leaving a note for her sleeping mother. Her mother already knew the plans for the day—that Clara, Gary, and Chris were driving up to Genesee for research for a school project. Knowing that her mother would assume Gary's parents would drive the kids, Clara didn't mention that Chris's brother would be driving them. The thought of this made her a bit nervous; she'd never met someone who'd served time in prison before.

Gary was ready to go when she arrived, a baseball cap tugged down over his unkempt hair.

After a few minutes of polite conversation with Gary's parents, a rusted Mustang pulled into the driveway and honked.

"That'll be the Becks," Gary said. "Love you, Mom. Love you, Dad. I'll see you tonight."

"Be back before eight!" Mrs. Mahler yelled as they went out the door.

Gary and Clara slid into the back seat as Chris introduced his brother.

"Hey guys, this is Micah," he said, gesturing grandly at the young man in the driver's seat.

"Buckle up, kids," said Micah. He had blond hair and the same blue eyes as Chris, but that was where the resemblance ended. His hair was close-cropped, and he had the beginning of a beard on his jaw. He wore a blue flannel shirt with the sleeves rolled up, and when he turned the steering wheel hard, Clara could see an arrow tattooed on the underside of his forearm.

At first, they drove in silence, and then Micah asked, "What do you kids need to do up in Genesee?"

"We have to do research. For a project," Gary said, repeating the vague excuse they'd all agreed on.

"Ha!" Micah said, seeing right through him. "Is that what you told your folks?"

"That is…literally what I told my folks, yes."

Micah laughed again. "And what are you really doing?"

"We read about a woman whose daughter went missing twenty-nine years ago," Clara said, "and she lives in Genesee. When we called her she said she wanted to talk to us in person."

Micah raised his eyebrows, glancing in the rearview mirror. "I guess that's one way to spend a Sunday."

"Micah's going there anyway, so he can meet with a dealer," said Chris. When he noticed Clara's shocked expression, he added, "No, not a drug dealer—a *gun* dealer."

Clara's mouth dropped open.

"Weapons dealer, actually. I gotta sell my knives, on account of I'm not allowed to own them at the present time," Micah said, with some bitterness.

He seemed to particularly like the next song that played on the radio, because he turned up the volume for the rest of the trip.

On the phone Sally Fahren had told them she would have time to talk in between the breakfast and lunch rushes, and when Micah finally dropped them off at a small retro-looking diner, Clara and the boys found it nearly empty.

"Thanks, Micah. See you in an hour!" Chris said.

"Or two," Micah responded, driving off.

The Deck was a small, family-owned establishment with small tables covered with cheerful gingham tablecloths.

The woman behind the counter looked tired, but not nearly old enough to be Sally.

"You'll be wanting to speak to my mom," she said, curtly, after Clara introduced herself. "And let me just go on record saying I don't think this is a good idea. Whatever happened to Jenny happened a long time ago. Good, bad, the worst—it don't matter. It's done." Then she disappeared into the kitchen to fetch her mother.

"Oh, look at you!" A woman who could only be Sally Fahren emerged from the kitchen, wearing an apron, wiping her hands on a red kitchen towel. "You must be Clara," she said, shaking Clara's hand, a smile lighting up her face. "And which one of you is Gary?"

"That's me," he said, and she shook his hand too.

"I see that you run on the Prairie Dale track team in the spring," she said. "Good job there. I looked you guys up on the internet. But I can't find anything on the internet about you, Chris," she said, wagging a finger in admonishment. "Now, skinny guy like you, you ever thought about maybe wrestling?"

For once, he was at a loss for words. "I…just joined the scholastic bowl team?"

"Well, I guess that's something. Have some school spirit, stay in school, go to college, get yourself a degree, and don't work at a dang greasy diner for your entire dang life. That's my advice. Now, how can I help you?"

"I hope we're not bothering you—" Clara began.

"There are a lot of things that bother me," Sally said, "but talking about my daughter's not one of them."

"We just want to know more about what happened," Gary said.

So Sally Fahren told the story. About how her daughter— her beautiful, shy, and thoughtful daughter—started acting strangely shortly after her fifteenth birthday. How she had spent hours in her room at first, and then had spent hours, then days, outside the house, gone who knew where.

"I never knew when I would see her next," explained Mrs. Fahren. "Of course, teenagers change. But not like this. Not Jenny. She was really a quiet girl. A loner. She loved to read. And she loved her momma. Once she came home soaking wet. Her hair, her clothes, everything. I asked her where she'd been. She said she'd been swimming in the lake. In February! It was nearly freezing. Of course, after she was gone, they checked the lake. Dragged the whole thing. She wasn't there."

"What can you tell us about...Theodore Herald?" Clara asked.

"That's the drifter the police were looking for. Yeah. Theodore. I met him once. He was in the store down where the gas station used to be. Other people saw him around. I guess he did a lot of yard work, odd jobs."

"Was he friends with Jenny?" Clara asked.

"I don't think so...Brandy Fredericks' girl did say that she saw them once after school, but everyone knows you can't trust the Frederickses. You know what I'm saying?"

Gary nodded.

Must be a small-town thing, Clara thought.

"I didn't realize at first she was gone," Sally continued, her voice quiet. "I thought she was just out running around for a day or two, like she'd started doing, but after the third day I called the police. They were no help. They thought she ran away, or that she'd killed herself. But girls who run away take stuff with them. She didn't take anything other than the clothes on her back."

"I was curious where she was last seen," Clara asked. "The newspaper didn't say."

Sally Fahren was thoughtful. "Let's see. The police say the last person to see her...to see her...was at the museum. The history museum. You know, on Knox Street. She had a part-time job there and stopped to pick up her check. But she never cashed it. It was like she'd vanished into thin air."

"What did you do with her stuff?" Chris asked, the first time he'd piped up.

"I kept her room exactly as it was for a while," she said. "After a few years, we boxed up all her things and made the room into an office. That was a hard day."

"Did you sell her things?" Chris asked.

"No. We donated some stuff to Goodwill, though. Clothes, a bed, her record albums and books. But now that I think about it, there was one thing that was missing. I haven't thought about it in years. There was a book."

Clara cocked her head. "What kind of book?"

"Oh, nothing—nothing special. It was like an old diary or a journal. She carried it with her everywhere for the last few weeks before she disappeared."

"I didn't read about that in the newspaper," Clara said.

"To be honest, I didn't even think about it at first. So much was going on. Then one night I couldn't sleep and I remembered how once or twice I caught her staying up past bedtime, reading that old book, and I thought, I wonder where that book went to?"

"Didn't the police ask if she had a diary? I mean, maybe she wrote about Theodore Herald or somebody in it." Gary did not want to give up on the Theodore Herald angle.

Sally made a face. "Oh, I don't think she would have written about him. Or anybody. It was a diary, but it wasn't *her* diary. It was some kind of antique book that she found."

The hairs stood up on the back of Clara's neck. "*Where* did she find it?"

"In one of the farmhouse walls, of all places. Someone made a hole and then patched it up with bricks, a long time ago."

Clara glanced at the boys, who were clearly as stunned as she was. Thinking about the implications of this news, she recited the facts in her head.

If Tad Trumpeter was actually Theodore Herald—she was 99 percent certain this was true—and if Theodore Herald had kidnapped or killed Jenny Fahren—she was 90 percent certain of this—and if the "diary" Jenny had found was a book of writings of Constance Love—there was at least an 80 percent chance of this—that meant Tad Trumpeter had gotten his hands on the predictions of the one woman who knew how to stop his massacre.

This was bad news.

They asked a few more questions, but Sally Fahren had no idea where Theodore Herald was from, or where he'd gone. She couldn't recall any specifics about the cover of the antique diary or a box it might have been originally stored in, and she had to get back to work soon.

"Thank you for talking to us," Gary said. "Would you mind if we called you if we think of any more questions about your daughter's death?"

The word dropped like a boulder. He'd meant to say *disappearance.*

"Oh no," Sally said. "Jenny's not dead. Heavens, no. My daughter's still alive. Something like this, a mother just knows."

Clara did the only thing she could think of to break the awkward silence that followed; she stood up and hugged the older woman, who hugged her back as if her life depended on it. Chris, who never seemed to think twice about social awkwardness, stood up and offered a hug too, after which Gary didn't want to be the odd one out.

"I don't want to keep you too long," Sally said, which in Illinois usually meant, *I don't want you to keep me too long.*

"We should probably get going," Clara agreed, and the boys mumbled assent as they put on their jackets.

Sally walked back toward the counter to check on the kitchen, and then she turned around. "Oh, there's one more thing I want to tell you," she said, gently. "When you get home, you find your parents, you tell 'em you love 'em, okay?"

Later, while they waited for Micah to pick them up, Gary took out a copy he'd sketched of the illustration of boxes and figures from Book Two.

"I think I know what this is! Here, turn it on its side."

"It's a map!" Chris said. With the page turned horizontally, Clara could almost see how this might be true.

"Or buildings, at least," Gary said.

"So maybe this is us," Clara pointed to the three figures, "and the star must refer to something important, like X marks the spot, right? But what building is it in? If this is a map, it's definitely not to scale."

"Wait a minute," Gary said. "That circle. I think I know what that building is. It's...the old colony administration building, on the edge of town. It's over a hundred years old, and its foundation was part of the original colony. It was totally in disrepair, and they...they built this new facade in the 1970s when they renovated it. It's got this weird modern circular doorway."

"How do you know all this?" Chris asked.

"They turned it into the history museum," Gary said. "My mom has to go there sometimes for meetings."

"I *thought* I had seen this somewhere before!" Clara said excitedly, as she took out the postcard on which their to-do list had been written. On the flip side was a photo of a building that looked as though a section of a massive round culvert had been stuck onto its doorway: the Henry County History Museum.

The last place Jenny Fahren had been seen before she disappeared.

30

The sectional championship for scholastic bowl took place on the following cold Saturday. It had drizzled overnight, so everything was damp. Mrs. Maynard booked one of Prairie Dale Middle School's two large vans, usually reserved for athletic teams, and she met the students just after dawn in the school parking lot.

During the drive, Mrs. Maynard turned the radio to a classical station, the best music, she said, to exercise young brains. Edison dozed, his head against the window, and Kaitlyn and Myron, sharing earphones, listened to music on Kaitlyn's iPod. Clara, Gary, and Chris were in a funk, having spent the last few days searching for any clue to the location of Constance Love's final resting place. They couldn't agree on what to do next. They had the text of the incantation from the book in Mr. Froehlich's classroom; they had Clara (and, thus, her blood). They had a rough idea of where the sepulchre was located (at the history museum, "where the Disappearing Girl of Biskopskulla was last seen"). They needed the bones of Constance herself, and time was running out.

Genesee Junior High School, the host of the tournament, was about three times the size of Prairie Dale and had about three times as many students. It was housed in a single, sprawling one-story building, constructed in the early 1970s from mottled brown and tan bricks. The teams gathered in the cafeteria as they arrived, and each school claimed a long table with bench seats as their home base for the day.

Most of the students in the room were strangers. A girl from the Genesee team came over to talk to Kaitlyn, and Gary decided to cheer up his friends (and himself) by doing opposition research on the other teams. This involved introducing himself to the person at each table who looked the least shy and asking if they had any gossip about the other schools.

Clara walked around the cafeteria. There was a long window with a counter at one end, covered by a padlocked metal grate. *That must be where hot lunches are served.* Two large cork boards lined one wall. Big, rounded letters above one of them proclaimed "SCHOOL EVENTS," and above the other, "COMMUNITY EVENTS." On the school events board she saw that Genesee High's drama club would be performing *Fiddler on the Roof* in two weeks.

Under community events, two flyers mentioned Biskop-skulla. One was an out-of-date advertisement for the Haw-ley Douglas Crazy Bomber 5K. The other was a brochure announcing the Henry County Heritage Festival. This year it was to focus on the settling of Biskopskulla. The event promised to have snacks from the nineteenth century and lots of fun one-room schoolhouse activities, culminating in a concert featuring dozens of grade-school children from all over the county singing songs written by early Biskopskulla settlers. "Recently discovered hymns!" exclaimed an off-cen-ter text box in Comic Sans font. "World premiere!" Even if the event hadn't been clearly aimed at younger kids, Clara knew she couldn't attend. It was scheduled for December 21, the same day as the winter solstice. One way or another, she and her friends would be otherwise occupied.

Gary came back to Prairie Dale's table and gestured to Clara. He gathered his teammates in a huddle, doing his best bad imitation of a football player before a big game. "Okay, guys, first of all, we're awesome and we are going to slay today—"

Chris let out a cheer in sarcastic falsetto: "Woohoo! Yay!"

"Second of all," Gary continued. "Let's not get our hopes up. We have absolutely no chance of winning."

Chris continued his high-pitched cheer. "Go team! Good speech!"

Kaitlyn looked at Gary with a mixture of affection and annoyance. "Gary, the *onus* is on each of us to keep a positive attitude."

"The onus is on us?" Gary said. "I like it! Anyway, here's the best intel I've got. Everybody here is good. But the most good—"

"The goodest?" said Chris.

"The absolute goodest," continued Gary, "is Sterling. They have a pair of ringers who transferred in last year. Divya and Darsh Pathak. Between the two of them, they know every fact that is humanly possible to know."

"That is definitely not plausible," Kaitlyn said.

"Literally, every fact possible. Also," Gary added, "Divya can do calculus in her head. Everyone seems to think their parents have PhDs. Nobody knows why they moved to Sterling." He motioned toward a table on the opposite side of the cafeteria, where Sterling Middle School had gathered. In the middle of the gathering of nervous students, two dark-haired siblings sat side by side, each drinking a diet cola, looking as relaxed as could be.

"Are they twins?" Myron asked.

"I don't think so," said Gary. "Just psychic." Myron nodded as if this were an obvious truth. "As long as we don't hit them in the first round, we have a shot."

Clara looked over at Darsh and Divya. She hadn't seen them in action, but she had no reason to doubt the rumors Gary had heard. It must be nice to be the best at something, she thought. She knew she wasn't the best scholastic bowl competitor; she just enjoyed having something to do with her friends. Today's meet provided a welcome distraction from the problems that had troubled her all week.

Still, she couldn't put the mission out of her head. What if they *never* found the last piece of the puzzle, the bones of Constance? What would happen if they failed?

A buzz went up around the room as the tournament director arrived to post the day's schedule on the wall. Today was to be a single elimination tournament. That meant that a team would be out as soon as they lost one match.

A small crowd gathered around the schedule, which was printed on a sheet of printer paper and was impossible to read from more than a few feet away. Chris managed to worm his way to the front of the pack and back to his team.

"Who do we hit?" Kaitlyn asked. "I know it won't be Genesee because we're both from the same region."

"Nope!" Chris said. "We get to face off in a sudden-death match with Sterling." Gary groaned. Chris added, "Woohoo! Go team!"

The Prairie Dale students got to the classroom first. Mrs. Maynard was needed to moderate a match in another part of the building, so it was just Edison, Kaitlyn, Myron, Gary, Clara, and Chris. The moderator, a tall gray-haired man wearing a John Deere jacket over an Oxford shirt and tie, arrived at the same time as the Sterling team. There were eight of them in total, and in addition to Divya and Darsh—the Pathak siblings—there were three boys and three girls.

Two tables had already been set up, with five chairs apiece and buzzers in the front of the room. The moderator, who introduced himself as Mr. Turner, moved his podium to the side and pulled a chair with attached desk into its position.

"I hope you guys don't mind if I sit. The ol' back has been killin' me this morning."

None of the students on either team minded.

Sterling dominated the first half of the match. It was pretty obvious why other teams on the circuit considered Divya and Darsh to be ringers: there seemed to be nothing they didn't know, and even when the questions were easy enough that another competitor might have the answer, they were still often able to buzz in first.

The question packets for this tournament included two algebra toss-up questions per match, and while the Prairie Dale students frantically copied the equations as the moderator read them, the Sterling students sat silent, not wanting to distract Divya, who always seemed to be able to buzz in with the correct answer as soon as the moderator finished the question.

It wasn't a total blowout. Myron was the first to answer a question about the location of the Triangle Shirtwaist Factory Fire (New York City), and that delivered a bonus question about volcanos that Edison and Gary fielded. One of the Sterling team members buzzed in too early on a question about Mary Shelley's *Frankenstein* and didn't realize that the answer sought was actually the subtitle of the novel, not the title. Clara managed to come up with *The Modern Prometheus* just in time.

When the clock had almost run out on the first half of the game, Sterling was up by 150 points. Gary, who had accurately predicted this thrashing, was still annoyed.

"In Korean folklore," began the final toss-up question of the match's first half, "this animal lives on the moon, making rice cakes. In every continent except Antarctica, they are found in the wild, and kept as both pets and livestock. Once categorized in the order *Rodentia*, they—"

Gary buzzed in. "Gary?" said Mr. Turner.

"The rat," Gary said.

"I'm sorry, that's incorrect."

Gary made a face as Mr. Turner finished reading the question. "Once categorized in the order Rodentia, they were moved into a new order, Lagomorpha, in 1912. Name this herbivore."

Darsh buzzed in. When he was called upon, he said, "Rabbit," and looked at Gary almost apologetically. It was the correct answer.

"Just one more reason to hate rabbits," Gary said under his breath.

At halftime, Chris subbed in for Gary.

During the two-minute break between halves, Edison walked over to the Sterling team.

"You guys are doing really great today," he said.

Divya smiled shyly. "Thanks! Your team seems like a really cool group."

Clara overheard the conversation and was struck by how pleasant the exchange was. She wasn't sure what tone, exactly, she expected between two rival teams, but it was nice to know that students from different schools could be pleasant to each other.

When the match started up again, Sterling answered four toss-up questions in a row, plus three of the ensuing bonus questions, solidifying their lead. At this point, it was a rout, and soon it would be mathematically impossible for Prairie Dale to make up the point deficit.

Clara didn't care that much about winning, but she appreciated the diversion that the competition provided, and she was disappointed that her team would likely be out of the tournament within minutes.

"The basic laws of this were first discovered by Leonardo da Vinci in 1493 and then rediscovered by Guillaume Amontons in 1699," began Mr. Turner. "There are four types of this: static, sliding, rolling, and fluid. It explains an object's surface resistance to—"

Clara buzzed in.

"Friction," she said, after she was recognized, earning her team the next bonus question.

"Throughout much of history, humans have accused each other of being witches. For ten points each—" Mr. Turner read. "First. One of the most famous witch trials in history took place in Salem, Massachusetts, from 1692-1693. One accused witch was pressed to death with heavy weights. How were the others executed?"

Kaitlyn whispered, "Burned at the stake, right?"

Chris's eyes widened in surprise. "NOOO!" he whispered. "Let me answer!" Kaitlyn nodded.

"They were hanged by the neck until dead," he said loudly.

"I'll take that. They were hanged," said the moderator. "Second. One famous English play features three weird sisters who chant in unison, 'Double, double toil and trouble; fire burn, and cauldron bubble.' Name that play."

Kaitlyn didn't wait for anyone. "*MacBeth*!" she said, excitedly.

"You're going to have bad luck now," Myron whispered.

"Very good," Mr. Turner said. "Okay. Three. In the eighteenth century, in order to prevent them coming back from the dead, suspected witches in Europe such as Meg Shelton and Lilias Adie were buried upside down with what object above them?"

Kaitlyn gave her teammates a questioning look. "Anybody?"

Edison wrote DEAD ANIMAL? on his scratch paper.

"Maybe they planted a tree above them?" Myron suggested.

Time was running out. Kaitlyn pointed to Clara. "It was your toss-up. You should decide this one."

"I need an answer." The moderator gave the required prompt.

"A…crucifix," Clara said.

"I'm sorry, that's not correct." After the Sterling team failed to answer, the moderator said, "I would have taken 'a boulder' or a 'stone slab.'"

Clara dropped her pencil. It bounced off the edge of the table and rolled away on the floor.

She was unable to focus for the rest of the match.

Prairie Dale failed to answer any more toss-up questions. That meant they were out of the tournament. The team was required to stay until lunch, because Mrs. Maynard was committed to help moderate for the rest of the morning.

As soon as she could, Clara pulled Chris and Gary aside.

"You guys," she said. "I think I know where they buried her."

She shared her theory.

"Brilliant," Chris said.

And Gary said, "We're going to need shovels."

31

The plan was to say that Constance was visiting relatives in Chicago, but in truth she made her way to Springfield. Mary worried nightly that Constance would run out of money and go hungry—she was such a naïve girl, after all—but Constance always managed to have a few dollars at the ready. When traveling, if there was ever anything of value by the side of the road, Constance would find it. Occasionally she would politely ask a stranger for a half-dollar; no one ever turned her down. In the city, when she encountered a game of chance, she could always win a small sum. She would find a man willing to take the money of a modestly dressed young woman, place one bet, and clap her hands like a child when the cards were dealt or the roulette wheel was spun. After she'd won, she would take her winnings, thank the man profusely, and refuse all entreaties to try her luck again.

Constance knew that she would attract only scorn if she showed off her gift (for that is how Thaddeus, the man with one blue and one black eye, persuaded her to view her visions: as a gift.) She avoided winning too much, and now that she was in Springfield, she avoided going into her trancelike state—when a detailed and far-ranging vision washed over her—unless she was safely locked in her hotel room.

Thaddeus had become her friend. He saw her in a way that no one in her life had ever seen her—as a person with great potential. He had also taught her a great deal about her gifts. How to use them. When to hide them.

She noticed one day that she had difficulty predicting his future. Her visions were never perfect, but with concentration, she could usually form some image in her mind. A piece of the future, if not the whole thing.

But Thaddeus was becoming hazy. The further into the future she tried to peer, the more invisible he became. Eventually Constance realized this meant he was taking steps to hide himself from her. What was he planning? She became increasingly suspicious of his motives and began to realize that his vision of the world was irredeemably different from her own. She couldn't forgive him, but she also couldn't tell anyone about what she knew.

One night, during her second week in exile, she woke up in her small room on the second floor of the third-best hotel in Springfield gasping for air. She didn't usually have visions while she was sleeping, but when she did, they were more elaborate, more colorful, and more powerful. She had seen a world that she didn't fully understand. It was her home, Biskopskulla, but it was different. People wore strange clothes and had curious hairstyles, and their manner of speaking to each other was odd. She had often assumed that her life would be short. Now she saw herself as a character in a much larger drama, in a life-and-death struggle that had lasted centuries, and would last for several more.

The next day, she bought several books from a local artisan. They were leather-bound, handmade blank books, and they were the same size as the journal she'd been writing in for years. Every night when she slept, she guided her own dreams, using her skill to peer into a distant future she could never live to see. In body, she remained a young woman, but in her mind, she aged unimaginably. Every morning, she filled her books with writing. Occasionally she drafted letters to her sister and brother-in-law. She knew they would worry, and that sharing trivial details about her circumstances would comfort them. One day she drafted a special letter to her sister, a letter that she sealed inside an envelope inside another envelope because it was urgent and confidential. Mary must visit at once, and she must visit alone.

Constance looked down at her growing belly. She could no longer ignore it. This problem required a sister's help.

32

The year was 1984. Regina Farber now lived in Chicago, having taken a job as an assistant museum curator. She didn't mind city life, although her apartment was tiny. Someday, she figured, she'd get fed up and move back to a small town.

Regina arrived at home with a stack of books, having stopped at a branch of the Chicago Public Library after work. She was a little shaken. Walking to her building from the train station in the dark, she thought she heard someone following her. The sidewalk was mostly empty, because the shops and restaurants in her part of town had closed for the night. She heard footsteps behind her that got closer and closer. She stopped.

The footsteps stopped.

She walked again, faster. For a moment, there were no suspicious sounds, and then—she heard someone running toward her from behind.

"Back off!" she yelled, spinning around.

There was no one there. Had the person ducked into the alley? Was it all in her head?

"I'm warning you," she said, loudly. "I've got an electric cattle prod, and I'm not afraid to use it!"

She didn't, of course, have a cattle prod. It was just the first weapon she could think of. After that, her walk home was uneventful. She thought perhaps she should look into getting a cattle prod, if it had such an effect on hoodlums.

Once inside, she locked the door. She sat down to read, a cup of tea beside her, and looked at the heap of books in front of her. She opened a book about the history of commerce in Springfield.

She was almost halfway through when she recognized the markings. Bold circles, drawn by hand above individual letters. She was used to this now. She'd encountered this many times before, although she had never told anyone about it—not even her closest friends.

She went to her filing cabinet and took out a folder containing pages and pages of notes. Then, curious, she checked the publication date on the copyright page of the book: 1953. Wow. This was the most recent book to contain the symbols.

But—of course! This wasn't like the previous times. The symbols—the code—hadn't been drawn directly onto the pages of the book. The page she was looking at contained photographs of signs in late nineteenth-century Springfield. Someone had defaced these signs in the 1860s, and then a photographer snapped pictures of them in 1902, and then an editor found them in an archive and included them in the book.

WESTERN SPRINGFIELD ILLINOIS BANK, read one. PUBLICK HALL - ENTRANCE OUT BACK, read another. There were symbols above eight of the letters: W-E-L-L-B-E-O-U-T.

As had become her tradition, she transcribed the letters onto the same sheet of notebook paper on which she'd written the very first strange message, "FARBER!" Many more lines had been filled, and she wrote the new letters, "WELL-BEOUT" directly underneath the letters written six months ago: "WELLJUST."

Well, be out! Well be out. We'll be out.

She flipped through the rest of the book to see if there were any more strange marks or symbols. There weren't, but she expected this. There never were. This was how it always went. She was curious, of course, but she had long ago made peace with the fact that this mystery would never be easily solved.

Regina Farber didn't believe in magic. But magic, she thought, somewhat irrationally, seemed to believe in her.

33

The body was buried in the front yard. It had to be. The kicker, for Clara, was the cemetery worker's memory of his father engraving the *Bed and Breakfast* inscription on the boulder. That meant the boulder had been used as an advertisement for only twenty years. But it had been in the yard long before that—Clara knew this because of the watercolor painting she'd made in art class. She'd used, as a model, a photo that was eighty years old, and the huge rock had been present in that photo.

Had it originally served a different, darker purpose?

The words of the scholastic bowl moderator echoed in Clara's head as she looked for shovels and trowels in the shed behind the house. *A boulder*, or *a stone slab*.

Clara was enthused. This was the best lead yet as to the location of Constance Love's remains. She thought about another phrase from the bonus question: *in order to prevent them coming back from the dead*. Were the Biskopskulla villagers really that superstitious? Did they worry that the woman they'd killed might come back to life?

During art class that week, Gary pointed out that if the villagers were superstitious enough to believe in witches, then they were certainly superstitious enough to believe that they might rise from the dead.

"That's a good hypothesis," Chris said. "But in point of fact, she *was* a witch. So the villagers were pretty much spot on."

The timing was crucial. The winter solstice, December 21, would fall on a Wednesday. This also happened to be one day after the end of the fall semester at Prairie Dale Middle School. Clara knew she'd never get permission to mount an excavation in the front yard, and the importance of the dig would be impossible to explain—to her mother, or to anyone. As such, the trio needed an opportune night to work in the dark. The hoped to preserve some sod while they dug and use it to cover up the hole after they'd filled it back in.

It was Gary's idea to set up a tent to hide their activities from the road. Families with young children often put a tent up in their yard, to give the kids an outdoor camping experience with access to the bathroom or their bedroom if they got scared, so it wouldn't look out of place to anyone driving by.

Clara used the impending Christmas holiday as an excuse to grill her mother about her upcoming work schedule. The implication, Clara hoped, was that she needed privacy to complete some last-minute Christmas preparations. The benefit of this strategy was that it allowed her to be cagey and mysterious without attracting suspicion.

Unfortunately, the only overnight shift that Ms. Hutchins was scheduled to work was on December 20, just one day before the solstice. "That won't give us much time if things go south," Chris said. As luck would have it, because Ms. Hutchins was the lowest in seniority at the hospital, and because many of her coworkers took time off around the holiday, she was also scheduled to work a day shift on the 21st, so she planned to nap in the hospital break room between shifts. She wouldn't be home all night or the next day.

"Just this once," she'd told Clara. "And then we'll have some extra money for the holidays!" Clara did her best not to look relieved at this lucky turn of events.

The three kids spent some time arguing about how long it would take to dig far enough to find the buried bones. Gary thought it would take an hour and a half. Clara figured two hours. "Amateurs!" Chris shook his head. "You guys have never done any serious digging, have you? It takes forever. Always. *Forever.*"

Clara and Gary trusted implicitly that Chris had experience digging large holes.

"We'll be lucky if we get to the payload"—this was Chris's new favorite term for Constance's skeleton—"in six hours. And that's under present conditions. If it freezes before Tuesday…" He shook his head again. "If it freezes, it'll take all night and half the next day. We'd be out of luck." Fortunately, the weather had remained cool and unseasonably mild so far.

The last day of fall semester was mostly uneventful. Clara hugged her mother in the morning, knowing she'd be gone when she got home from school. She had passed all of her classes with good grades. She was especially proud of the A she'd earned in art class, in spite of the fact that there had been no homework and no tests.

In study hall she was surprised when Mrs. Maynard handed her a big green envelope on the way out the door, offered her a hug, and wished her Merry Christmas. "It has been wonderful making your acquaintance this semester, and I hope you know you are a delightful addition to the student body here!" Mrs. Maynard said. Clara was touched.

When she got to her locker, she opened the card. Inscribed in it was a quotation from Charlotte Brontë: *But life is a battle: may we all be enabled to fight it well!*

As she left school and prepared to meet her friends at dusk, she thought that her life here in Biskopskulla had become quite a battle indeed.

They broke ground just after eight p.m. Although they couldn't be certain all the neighbors were asleep, the sky was uniformly cloudy and black, and the tent Gary had set up in front of the dig to block their excavation site was big enough to house a family of five.

For equipment, they had two digging shovels with U-shaped grips, so they took turns. One person kept watch and made runs into the kitchen for caffeinated beverages while the other two dug.

It didn't take much time for Chris's prediction to prove

accurate: their progress was very slow. Chris and Gary took the first shift digging, and the mood was light and optimistic. After the first half hour, Clara took over for Gary, who then rotated in for Chris thirty minutes later.

They tried to dig a circular hole about five feet in diameter, centered around the place on the lawn where the boulder had been. After a few false starts, they realized that they needed to pile up the dirt from the hole much farther than they'd originally planned, to prevent it from sliding back toward the crater they'd created.

Clara found a small rusty wheelbarrow in the shed behind the house and set about moving the mound a few yards away.

After nearly three hours, the hole was just over two feet deep, and they had to step into the depression and dig from the inside.

Later, when Chris was sitting on the edge of the hole, they had a brief false alarm. "Whoa. Where did you get that?" Gary asked Chris, who was absentmindedly tapping two rather large, bone-shaped objects together.

"Uh, it was a birthday gift when I was twelve."

Clara looked more closely. Chris was definitely holding two bones, each about the length of a person's forearms. "Chris!" she said. "Did we miss something? Did you just find those?"

"No, they were literally a gift for my twelfth birthday. A pig skeleton. These are femurs, I'm pretty sure."

Gary blinked. "You just happened to have two...pig... femurs with you?"

Chris unzipped his duffel bag, revealing a large assortment of yellowish bones, including a rather frightening-looking pig skull.

"Just...carrying those around?" Gary said.

"Yeah, in case I got bored," Chris said. "And for luck."

"Chris, buddy. I don't pretend to understand you," Gary said, "but you are a truly unique individual."

Chris raised a pig femur to his forehead and saluted.

There were a few minor mishaps. Gary found gauze and taped up a blister on his hand, then tracked down two pairs of gloves to better protect their hands. Clara stood in the wrong place while Chris threw a shovelful of earth over his shoulder and got a face full of dirt. Chris nearly broke the blade of his shovel when he slammed it full force into a hidden rock. Still, they worked well together, and at least they were making some headway.

Then it started to rain. The temperature dropped dramatically, and the coats they were wearing did little to keep off the chill. Clara scrounged around inside for a sweatshirt that was big enough for Gary to use as an extra layer. Chris swore he didn't need one. Even worse, the ground became heavier. Each scoop, each wet shovelful, weighed twice what it had before. The going slowed down considerably.

By one in the morning, they were exhausted, and sore, and irritable. The crater was approximately five feet deep, and Clara realized with dread that she would never be able to make the lawn look unharmed. Too much of the pile of displaced dirt was turning into mud and sliding away.

She thought about the cataclysm, and the terrible dream she'd had. *I guess you can't make an omelet without breaking a few eggs*, she thought. *After all this is done, I might be locked in my room for the next six months. But if we don't succeed, I might not have a room to come home to.*

Chris stood up and stretched. With his feet at the bottom of the hole, now only the top of his shoulders were above the ground. His hair was sopping wet. He shivered. "No risk, no reward," he said quietly.

"No," said Clara. "You have to dry off and warm up. We'll do that in shifts. I'll take your spot for the next twenty minutes. Go inside."

Chris didn't protest, and Clara jumped down into the hole. Gary kept digging. To save his back, his new strategy was to scrape the top layer of soil to loosen it, then gather it up and throw it over his shoulder and out of the hole.

Clara soon found that the growing layer of water at the bottom of the hole made digging almost impossible. She couldn't see the surface of the dirt anymore, and the suction from the water rushing in when she tried to pull up a shovelful of earth made the whole process unbearable. Soon both she and Gary were carefully scraping just underneath the surface of the muddy water beneath them.

"Ugh," she said. "How do you feel?"

"Trying not to think about how badly everything hurts," Gary said. "Hoping Chris comes out to relieve me soon."

"Hopefully after tomorrow, this will all be over."

"Odds are that's gonna be true, one way or the other," Gary said, grimly.

In the distance, lightning flashed.

"Oh, perfect," Gary groaned. A few seconds passed, and then they heard the low rumble of thunder. "We have to finish this if a thunderstorm is coming. It isn't safe."

The two of them worked faster, trying to get as much done in the next few minutes as possible. "Did you drop something?" Gary asked.

"I don't think so. Why?" Clara asked.

"I keep hitting these...I don't know what they are. Wood pieces?" As Gary pushed his shovel through the water, it gathered up little floating objects, the size of dice.

Clara motioned to Gary to stop digging and squatted to look at them. "Bones," she said. "These are bones!"

"Don't get excited," Gary admonished. "Human bones don't float. This must be an animal, most likely a bird."

"Oh," Clara said, disappointed.

Still, she raked the floor of the crater, now under almost a foot of water, even more gently with her shovel. She could feel its smooth trajectory over the mud until it stopped abruptly at something hard.

She bent down to reach in and find out what it was, but just as her face got close to the surface of the dirty water, a grinning skull jumped up at her.

Clara screamed, then cut her own scream short when she realized it wasn't really jumping and it wasn't really grinning. It had merely floated up when she dislodged it, its jawbone miraculously intact.

"What the—?" Gary asked. "How is that even possible? It's bobbing like an apple."

From just above their heads, they heard a loud voice enunciating in a British accent. "WHAT FLOATS IN WATER?"

Gary grinned and looked up at Chris. "A witch!"

"I would also have accepted *bread* or *churches*," Chris said.

"Do you guys really think…" Clara struggled to formulate her thoughts. "Do you think this is floating because of magic, or because of some…congenital condition?"

"Does it matter?" Gary said. "You had a hunch Constance would be buried here, and we found…a lot of human bones. Come on. Let's try to get them all."

With renewed energy, Clara and Gary spent the next twenty minutes gathering bones and handing them up to Chris, who placed them unceremoniously inside a double garbage bag.

It would not have been an easy task under the best conditions, but at night, as the rainfall increased, with a lightning storm approaching, there was no way of knowing how much of the skeleton they managed to salvage. Clara was pretty certain she'd seen a number of finger bones, but the cartilage holding the bones together must have decomposed long ago.

CRACK! A flash of lightning struck the road in front of the house, and the thunderclap reached them almost instantly. "We've got to get out of here," Gary said. "We can't finish the spell if we're dead."

He tried to help Clara up the side of the crater, but it proved so slick that she fell back down. "Here," he said, making a step with his gloved hands. He boosted her toward Chris, who lay prone on the wet grass and pulled up on both of her arms. She managed to scramble up and out of the pit.

Gary was heavier than Clara, so she and Chris both lay

horizontally to let him use their arms for leverage as they pulled him up.

The wind picked up, and Clara shouted, "Get inside!"

Once they were all in the kitchen, Clara looked through Chris's garbage bags to see the bones they'd managed to salvage. "I'm gonna make three grilled cheese sandwiches," Gary said. "Anybody need anything else?"

Chris threw out his arms expansively. "A chalice of your finest pop! To celebrate the fact that we DID IT! We found all of the elements for the spell."

"I always knew we would," Gary said.

"I didn't," Chris said, opening a can of cola. "I just knew we had to try."

"All right, guys," Clara said. "We should eat and get some sleep. Big day tomorrow." She went to lock the front door. Lightning flashed, and the whole outdoors lit up. A few seconds later they heard thunder. The storm was moving away.

But something outside the window didn't seem right.

Clara motioned to the other two, and then whispered, "Guys!" when they didn't see her.

As they gathered around the window, Clara pointed to the park up the street, a block away, where she thought she'd seen a person standing. Lightning flashed again. There was a man outside, about ten feet closer than he'd been before. He was standing dead still, looking right at Clara's house.

The sky lit up once more, and the man was another ten feet closer. They hadn't seen him move at all, but somehow in the darkness he progressed toward them. His face was hard to make out, but at the next flash of lightning, his hands, and the one glove he wore, were visible.

It was Tad Trumpeter. And they all were certain that he was coming for them.

When the sky lit up again, he was on the street in front of the house. It was time to run, to hide, to do…something.

34

An oriel window was a common feature in Victorian architecture. This is a window that projects outward from the second story of a house, like a bay window. According to the chapter "Painted Ladies" in Regina Farber's book *A Preservationist's Guide to Small-Town Illinois*, these windows allowed residents to remain hidden, yet still see what mischief was occurring on the street or lawn below. When Tad easily opened the locked front door of the former bed and breakfast, Clara, Gary, and Chris were watching from the oriel window. If he proceeded upstairs, there would be nowhere to go but the roof. If he went down to the basement, they would have a chance to run down to the back door.

They heard the front door slam behind him as Tad entered the house. He wasn't trying to be secretive. He wanted to frighten them.

The three of them waited, not breathing, until Clara heard the familiar creak of the basement stairs. It would be obvious within seconds that they weren't down there; they had to go *now*. They ran down the stairs to the first floor, but while Chris and Clara sprinted through the living room toward the back door, Gary ran to lock the basement door.

When Gary got to the door, Tad was already on his way back up the stairs. Seeing the boy at the top of the stairs, he bellowed and bounded upward. Gary slammed the door and locked it just as Trumpeter reached the top and threw his weight against the door.

By the time Gary got outside, he could hear the door crack. In another moment, it would break open.

Where were Clara and Chris? Gary looked left and right. What were the obvious hiding places? To his left, he could see a plastic playhouse in another neighbor's backyard. Then he caught sight of his friends waving at him; they'd been watching the back door from behind a garage, back at the edge of the property. He scrambled in their direction as he heard the door break open inside the house.

Garages in this part of town were old freestanding painted wood structures, converted from what had originally been storage sheds, barely big enough to hold one car.

Once Gary caught up to them on the opposite side of the garage, Chris said, "Get inside; our only chance is to hide."

The garage had a dirt floor. It was only about eight feet tall and it was being used to store junk. Packed almost to the ceiling with broken furniture and sagging cardboard boxes, Clara's grandmother—or perhaps a previous owner—had cleared a narrow corridor down the middle. A bare light bulb hung from a chain on the ceiling, but none of them dared pull it for fear Tad might notice. Chris and Gary tried to quietly look around to see if they could find anything useful. Clara found a narrow crack between two boards and peered through to see if she could spot Tad Trumpeter. She could only fit one eye up against the crack, and it took her a moment to focus. At first she couldn't find him anywhere. Then she saw that he was still standing in the backyard; apparently, he'd decided there was no point in running after them if he didn't know which way they had gone.

Clara felt sick. Tad wasn't armed—not that she could see, at least—but he was still the most intimidating man she had ever encountered. She tried not to think about all the innocent people that he must have killed over the many years he'd been alive.

Then Tad did something strange. He took a leather pouch out of the black jacket he was wearing. He unzipped the pouch, rummaged in it with two fingers for a moment, and pulled out a tiny white object. From this distance, Clara couldn't tell what it was. It was about the size of a postage stamp, and it seemed to weigh almost nothing.

Tad placed the object in the air in front of him. It hovered there, motionless. He whispered something to it, and it began floating around. It veered left and right, and even circled back on itself a few times, but it gradually drifted in the direction of the old shed where Clara and the boys were hiding.

At first Tad just watched as it wafted away from him, then he followed it, with slow, confident steps. As it got nearer, Clara could see that the object was a feather. By the time it had halved the distance between the house and the shed, she realized it was too late. She pulled away from the crack and gestured to Gary and Chris to be silent.

"He's using magic to find us," she whispered. "Find something to defend yourself with. Maybe we can overpower him."

Gary found a pair of sturdy chair legs. He lifted one and gave Chris the other one.

Clara considered a wooden coat hanger, then rejected it in favor of a long narrow piece of wood lined with ridges, which looked like the bottom ledge of an old chalkboard. When she picked it up, she knocked over a shoebox full of moldy papers. The clatter wasn't loud, but still Gary gasped.

Clara returned to spying out of the crack and saw that Tad was nearly upon them. At least he seemed to be, but the hovering feather veered backward and then away from them, toward the neighbors' house. Tad followed it, and for a split-second Clara thought it would guide him away from them. But then the feather darted around the side of the shed like a lightweight bullet, and Tad's eyes fixed on their hiding place as though he knew exactly how to interpret the feather's movements.

Gary looked for a way to lock the door—a good idea, but too late. The door flung open, seemingly of its own accord. Tad stood outside the shed, placing something inside his coat. Clara realized he was returning his enchanted feather to the leather pouch. He held a thin green candle burning with a strange flame.

Gary's right foot moved, knocking against a wooden crate, and Tad turned his head toward the sound. Tad pinched the wick of the candle, and somehow Gary's movements slowed as if he were wading through concrete.

Clara tried to speak, but Tad blew gently on the candle's flame and it burned higher.

"Hush, girl. I don't know what spells she might have taught you in that book of hers, so I'm afraid I can't let you speak."

They were trapped. Paralyzed. Clara noticed that Chris was straining so hard against his incapacitation that the veins on his temples were twitching.

Tad moved so that his frame filled the doorway. He calmly cast his gaze upon each of them in turn. Clara had never felt so terrified. They were face to face with the enemy, and they were sitting ducks.

In the distance, the new church bell could be heard. Tad looked annoyed. "I don't have time to deal with you, but I can't have you interfering today. Sit tight, little ones." With that, he slammed the shed door shut and locked it. They heard a great thud, as if something heavy had fallen against the front of the shed.

As soon as Tad was out of sight, Gary fell forward toward the door and Clara very nearly collapsed. She realized that her ability to move had returned, and she wondered for a split-second if she could talk now, too.

To test it, she screamed at the top of her lungs.

Outside the shed, no one heard.

35

G od have mercy on me, Constance, for what I am about to do," Mary said, gripping her sister's arm tightly and pulling her out of the house toward the tool shed fifty yards away.

It had been several months since Constance returned to the colony of Biskopskulla, and one more since Mary had returned with her newborn, a perfect, healthy baby girl. Mary and Carl's hopes that the colony's animosity toward Constance would fade in her absence had been dashed. Shortly after Constance's return, a wild-eyed old woman from the old country blamed Constance for the disappearance of two twins. It was as if the entire population was stricken with some mysterious illness, Mary said, a mania directed irrationally at Constance.

"I think," Constance replied, "that may be more true than you know."

"Hide," Mary said. "If they find you, they will surely kill you."

"They will kill me," Constance agreed, "after they find me in the morning."

"I beg you to stop your prophesies, sister. I'll come back after the searchers have gone. You may yet escape to our uncle's farm in Wethersfield. He can take you to Chicago, and you can find work there."

"Look at you, Mary." Constance's eyes softened as she gazed at her sister "You have grown up to be a fine woman. I didn't harm the Altona child," she added.

"Of course you didn't," Mary said, pushing her further into the dark shed. "Now, sister, hide."

Constance didn't look at her. "You're needed in the house," she said, sounding worried, and Mary ran off.

It was a lie. Mary wouldn't be needed for another hour. But it was Constance's last chance to test her sister, to see if she really believed in her. It gave her some small comfort, in her last hours, to know that Mary couldn't ignore an urgent prediction. And it might do Mary some good, if she felt that this last prediction was wrong. She could believe her sister was crazed after all, not a witch.

Alas, neither was entirely true. Constance wasn't particularly crazy, and she was, in a manner of speaking, a witch. She placed a hand on the sharpened tools hanging in front of her and selected a small hand drill. She chose a board in the back of the shed and began to drill a tiny hole in the hard wood. She drilled as quietly as she could. When she had bored a hole almost through the board, she began to drill another hole, a fraction of an inch away.

She kept this up, without resting, for the next four hours. She drilled with only a tiny drill bit, barely thicker than a needle. She made indentations up the entire length of the board, standing on her toes to finish near the top. She stopped when she heard shouting in the house. They were coming for her. She knew what came next. But there was one thing left to do.

She found an awl, thicker than the drill, and carved directly onto the wood surface, as quickly and deeply as she could. She mimicked an illustration from her schoolbooks—an ear here, a paw here—and she finished just as the Spencer boys swung open the door.

She hadn't thought to barricade it or even lock it, but it wouldn't have mattered. They would have gotten her in the end.

She blew away the wood shavings on the wall to reveal a rather lopsided rabbit. In the years to come, condensation would drip down the hard walls of the shed, collecting in the minuscule indentations where her tools had carved the wood away.

"It will have to do," she said, as they seized her forcefully and pulled her from the shed to her execution.

36

It had been hours. At first, they took turns yelling for help. Clara's throat was sore and her voice was hoarse. She wished she had thought to grab her cell phone from the kitchen counter before she'd left the house, but there had been no time anyway.

Although they each tried many times to open the shed door, it was well and truly jammed. After they'd been trapped for some time—Clara estimated a good three or four hours, although she had no way of knowing for sure—Chris began hurling himself at the door, slamming against it with all of his weight. He looked as though he intended to smash himself to pieces, and it took both Clara and Gary to pull him away and calm him down.

"Do you think Tad has the bones?" Gary wondered, when they were all sitting down later.

"I mean..." Clara began. "Does he need them? They were for *our* spell, right, not his—whatever it is he needs for his enchantment. The *cataclysm*. I figured he was trying to find them to keep us from getting them, to keep us from stopping him. But now—" She looked around. "It looks like that's a nonissue."

Chris didn't look up from the floor. "He'd have to find them to get them. And I don't think he can use magic to find them. If he could, he would have done it a long time ago."

Clara looked puzzled. "Why would he need magic? We left the bag of bones in the middle of the kitchen."

Chris still didn't look up. "I...may have...put them in the bottom right drawer of your fridge. And when I say 'may have,' I mean I did."

"I can't believe you had enough time to hide them! We

barely got out of the house after Clara saw Tad," Gary said.

"No, Clara hadn't seen him yet. I just put them there when I was getting a drink out of the fridge."

"You put them in the *refrigerator*?" Clara asked, amazed. "Just…just because?"

"Seemed like a good place for 'em," Chris said, finally looking up and smiling.

"Never change," Gary said.

They grew hungry, but tried not to talk about it.

Gary fell asleep first. Clara and Chris gave each other a look as if to say, *Let's not wake him.* But it wasn't long before Chris's head started nodding, and soon he too was out.

All right, thought Clara, *I'll stay up. One of us has to stay awake, in case we hear anything.*

She lasted for twenty minutes.

When she woke up, Gary and Chris were whispering, keeping themselves entertained by telling each other horror stories they'd read in books growing up.

Gary looked at her. "She's up!"

"What time is it?"

"I don't know. It's still light outside, but I think the sun's going down," Gary said.

"It's the shortest day of the year, so it's going to come down quickly. You guys seem surprisingly calm."

"God grant me the serenity to accept the things I cannot change," Chris said, "the courage to change the things I can, and the wisdom to know the difference."

"I didn't know you prayed. Do you go to church?" Clara asked him.

"No, but I know a lot of alcoholics," he said truthfully.

There was a thin beam of light coming in from a gap between the front wall of the shed and the roof. In the past few minutes it had changed to a golden orange.

Clara looked up at the gap. "Do you think—?"

"We tried," Gary cut her off. "Chris stood on my shoulders. The roof wouldn't budge."

The angle of the light illuminated the rear wall of the shed.

A crude drawing of a rabbit was etched in the wood.

"Dang it," Gary said, "that's the last straw." He stood up. "My whole life...my whole life I spend wondering what things would be like if some stupid...*rabbit*...hadn't run out in the middle of the road. I could have had a big brother, except...except I wouldn't, because I wouldn't even *be here* if he hadn't died. You know, he was even born in the Year of the Rabbit? It's supposed to mean hope, but that's a lie." He cursed. "Those little monsters have been haunting me my whole life, any time something goes wrong. So it stands to reason," he stomped toward the back of the shed, "one of them would be here looking down on me at my lowest point."

He pointed. On the rear wall of the shed, plain as day, the image of the large rabbit was visible. It had been scratched into the wood like an etching, and there was a smoky black smear where its eyes should be. Clara shivered.

"It's watching us," Gary said. "This means we failed, and he's here"—he tapped the rabbit's forehead—"to bear witness."

Gary took a step back. Without warning, he lunged and punched the rabbit in the face, yelling as he did so. He punched again and again, until Clara shouted at him to stop.

"One more for good measure," Gary said. Ignoring the pain, he balled up his fist and slammed it into the rabbit's nose.

His hand broke through the wall of the shed. The tiny holes in the wooden board had collected moisture over decades and decades; tiny filaments of mold digested microscopic portions of hard wood until this part of the wall was no longer structurally sound.

"Holy—" Gary whispered as Chris sprang up.

"You broke the wall!" he shouted. As Gary stepped back and nursed his hand, Chris picked at the wood on the edges of the new hole. It crumbled beneath his fingers.

Clara handed him a chair leg, which he used to carve out the wood, to find the soft parts. Soon the hole was as big as his head, and in a few minutes it was just large enough for Chris to fit through. Because it was several feet off the ground, Clara and Gary helped boost him up to it. He ran around to unlock the door.

He quickly appeared back at the hole. "Okay, that won't work. There's a tree blocking the door. Hang on."

He ran away and came back in a few minutes with an axe. Clara didn't recognize it, but she figured the chances were about equal that he had found it in her house's tool shed or just brought it with him.

Chris was adept with an axe, and by the time he finished hacking an opening large enough for the other two to walk through comfortably, the sun was dangerously close to setting on the horizon.

There was indeed a tree flush against the door of the shed: a massive, living oak tree, with roots that stretched for several feet in three directions. Even if they'd managed to break the lock, they never could have pushed the door open.

"How did…that tree…?" Clara asked.

"I'm gonna assume magic," Chris said.

"Let's get our stuff," Gary said, nursing his hand. "We've got a job to do."

37

Chris and Clara were out of breath when they caught up to Gary at the Henry County History Museum. Because Gary was the fastest, he ran ahead and scoped out the museum. Based on the map, they figured they were looking for the lowest point in the building, a basement or subbasement. As she approached, Clara saw cars pulling into the parking lot and families with children getting out. At the large, circular doorway—gosh, it *was* a jarring addition to the building—an elderly man held the door open for a group of grade-school children. What were they here for? Clara saw a familiar flyer: *Henry County Heritage Festival*. Of course, some festival activities would take place at the museum.

The event was a mixed blessing. It meant that no one would wonder why a group of disheveled middle-school students were nosing around a museum that would otherwise be closed, but it also meant that there were people here to wonder what they might be up to.

A little girl wearing a bright green coat and high-top sneakers was holding the string of a silvery helium balloon. She looked about six years old. She kept looking up at her balloon as she walked, and she stumbled off of the edge of the sidewalk, nearly tumbling to the ground until a boy a few years older, who must have been her brother, caught her. The girl held on to his jacket, looked up to where Clara was standing, and waved shyly.

Clara smiled at her.

"What took you guys so long?" Gary asked. He had run the distance from Clara's house to the museum, over two miles, at top speed.

"Shut. Up," Chris managed between gasps.

"Okay," Gary said. "We need to go to the back. There's a door. It's not locked. There's some offices back there or something, and I could see some stairs down. Walk with me. Walk…with purpose. If anyone stops us, tell them we're volunteers. Say whatever you have to say. Do whatever you have to do."

"How much time do we have?" Clara asked.

"Not enough time. We're really cutting it close."

Clara should have been tired, but after the last twenty-four hours, she'd never felt so much adrenaline. "Guys, hurry. But try not to think about what will happen if we don't get there in time."

She looked out toward the horizon at the village buildings and wondered where Tad was now, and she wondered what kind of disaster the Baneful and Cursed One had planned.

38

The woman behind the heavy wooden desk glanced down at the soft ruled paper on her desk, now decades old, and at the typewriter where she had—for the final time—transcribed the contents of the older paper, the result of almost five decades of careful work. Some years she had stumbled across only part of a word; other years, a handful. But she'd returned to this document whenever she felt frustrated by life. In the last few months, it had become more of an obsession than a hobby, as she worried that she might die without ever sharing what she'd discovered.

She'd long since given up on the idea that she would figure out what it *meant*. Was it a poem? A message? The rantings of a lunatic? Did it matter?

She was about to put everything inside a folder, and put the folder inside an overstuffed handbag, when she heard them. "This way!" a boy's voice said.

Perhaps some children had gotten lost, or wandered away from the festival upstairs. It wouldn't be the first time that participants in an event at the museum's great hall had taken a wrong turn or gone exploring, and ended up in the archives.

She cleared her throat.

"There's someone here," another boy's voice said, softly.

"It's locked," said a girl's voice.

Enough was enough. The archivist got up from her desk, straightened up to her full height, and walked with a cane to locate the young trespassers.

She found three children, in their early teens by the look of it, who had wandered into the building and were now examining the basement's inner door.

"Gary, you didn't say there would be another door," the girl said.

"Uh, Clara," the taller boy said, with a hint of condescension, "I didn't know there *was* another door."

"I brought an axe," the other one said. He wore an ill-fitting backpack. "I can probably hack through it."

"Excuse me!" the archivist called out, louder than necessary. This startled the youths. "YOU WILL DO NO SUCH THING!"

"You can't go down there," she continued. "It isn't safe. No one has been down to the basement in years. It was locked up after it flooded. I don't even know if the electricity works down there. Anyway, you shouldn't be here. This part of the museum is closed now. Now run along, or I'll have to call the police."

The look of panic on each of their faces took her by surprise. She didn't expect this much fear and anguish from a group of kids. Almost in tears, they started babbling.

Chris squinted and read the name tag on her sweater. "Farber!"

"Look, ma'am," Clara implored, "I don't know how to explain. We have to go down there."

Gary grunted through gritted teeth, "*Volunteers!*"

Clara shook her head. "I'm just going to be honest. This is really important and you just have to trust us."

Chris added, "Look the other way. No one will know. We'll just—we'll be out of here before you know it."

Gary, ignoring the woman, said to Clara, "We could try a different place."

"There isn't a different place," Clara insisted. "It has to be here. We have to go through that door, down those stairs, and save the town." She looked at the woman, who was white as a sheet. "Please? Are...are you okay?"

Regina Farber looked very pale. Her eyes were wide, and she looked as if she were about to cry. She trembled involuntarily.

"I'm fine," she said. "Hang on!"

She walked deliberately back to her desk.

She looked at the paper still in the typewriter, and at the text she had finished transcribing just minutes earlier. These were the mysterious words she had been gradually encountering for most of her adult life.

FARBER! it began.
LOOK MAAM
I DON'T KNOW HOW TO EXPLAIN
WE HAVE TO GO DOWN THERE
VOLUNTEERS
IM JUST GOING TO BE HONEST THIS IS REALLY IMPORTANT
AND YOU JUST HAVE TO TRUST US
LOOK THE OTHER WAY
NO ONE WILL KNOW
WELL JUST (?)
WE'LL BE OUT OF HERE BEFORE YOU KNOW IT
WE COULD TRY A DIFFERENT PLACE
THERE ISN'T A DIFFERENT PLACE
IT HAS TO BE HERE
WE HAVE TO GO THROUGH THAT DOOR
DOWN THOSE STARES
AND SAVE THE TOWN
PLEASE ARE
ARE YOU
OH.

Regina swallowed. She opened the bottom drawer of the desk and retrieved a key ring thick with heavy keys. She located the key to the basement door and handed it to Clara.

"I think I was...always supposed to give you this," she said.

Clara looked surprised, but she didn't have time to ask questions. "Thank you!" Clara exhaled. "Thank you so much!"

As the three young people made their way down the basement stairs, Regina took a pen from the desktop and crossed out the final word, "OH," replacing it with "Okay."

Then she sat down, and she stared at it in fascination.

39

At the bottom of the basement stairs was another door. This one was unlocked, and when Clara threw it open, whatever lay beyond was enveloped in utter darkness. She fumbled for a light switch, pressing her hand against the inside wall.

"We should've brought a flashlight," Chris observed.

"We should've done a lot of things," Gary said, "but we were a little pressed for time."

Clara heard something move inside the basement as her hand passed over what felt like bricks, and she shuddered. She hoped nothing too disgusting was stuck to this wall.

"Got it!" she said, finding a light switch and flipping it.

There was a pop in front of them. For a second, nothing happened, and then a flickering incandescent light bulb lit up.

"I guess the electricity does work," Gary said.

In front of them was a hallway about twenty feet long. Cobwebs lined the junctions where the dirty brick walls met a low ceiling. The husks of many different species of insect lined the floor. At the end, the hallway turned a corner.

"Dead cockroaches. Fun," Chris said, walking out to the middle of the hallway. Then, as he watched a few of them scatter, "Ope, nope," he said. "A few of them are alive."

"Let's go," Clara said. They moved on to the end, where they turned the corner and found another light switch.

The new hallway was approximately the same length as the previous one, and twice as dirty. The doorway at its end was blocked by a stack of stained wooden boxes, each displaying the letters "HCD." They took positions on either side of the stack and quickly moved the boxes to the sides of the hallway, starting with the ones on top of the stack.

"Ohhhhh," whispered Chris, lifting a medium-sized box

at shoulder height. "This one's slimy. Why did it have to be slimy?" He wiped his hands on his pants and kept restacking boxes.

Once through the doorway, they walked down yet another hall. "At least it shouldn't be too hard to find our way back," Gary said. They found a light switch, but the bulb was burned out, so their way forward was particularly dim. They tried not to look down at the insect bodies crunching beneath their feet.

The hall opened out into a subterranean room, about thirty by fifty feet. At the far end were piles of blankets and stacks of old books. A single overhead bulb was already illuminated. Their attention was transfixed by what they saw in the middle of the chamber.

"I, uh, didn't expect it would be a *literal* altar," Gary said. "Did you?" The others shook their heads.

Standing dead in the center of the room was a carved wooden altar that looked as if it had been stolen from a country church. Angels and cherubs decorated its sides. The surface on top was perfectly smooth and clean.

"There's no dust," Clara said. "Why isn't there dust?"

"We don't have time," Gary pointed out. "We have to complete the spell before 4:23 p.m."

Clara looked at her phone. It was dead. "Might as well do it now," she said, "and hope it's not too late."

Chris opened up his backpack and pulled out the skull of Constance Love with one hand as if he were holding a bowling ball.

"You're not even wearing gloves?" Clara said.

"No time to be dainty," he said, placing the skull on the altar.

"No time, period," Gary said. "Give me that." He took the backpack and dumped it, unceremoniously, onto the altar. Removed from any context, it was hard to tell that an entire human skeleton was present. Ligaments still connected some of the finger bones to each other, and sections of the vertebrae were intact, but the overall impression was a jumble. It looked like the nest of some large predatory bird.

Chris turned to Clara. "*Blood of my blood*," he said. "Blood of *her* blood, anyway. You ready?"

Clara nodded. She took one of her grandmother's antique pearl-handled paring knives out of the zippered pocket of the backpack.

"Is that clean?" Gary asked.

"Is it sharp?" Chris asked.

"As far as I know, yes," she said. "I was rushing."

"Here," Chris said. He produced a match from one of his pockets and struck it rather artfully on the zipper of the backpack. He placed his hand over Clara's on the knife handle and slowly moved the match up and down the edge of the blade to sterilize it. When the flame on the matchstick got too close to his fingers, he blew it out.

"Where should I cut?"

"Fingertip?" Gary suggested. "Palm of your hand? That's how they do it in movies."

She lifted the knife and realized her hands were shaking.

The enormity of what they were doing hit her like a wave of cold water. The stakes were high: "Untold numbers" might die. But what they were doing, and what they were attempting to do…? This was *magic*. People died for this stuff. People killed for this stuff. Her great-great-great-grandmother had learned that the hard way.

On top of all that, she'd lied to her mom.

Ugh, you're not being rational, she thought. She was having trouble thinking clearly. There was a buzzing noise overhead, and then something that sounded like distant clapping. Her face was turning white.

"Clara, you okay? Do you get freaked out by blood, is that it?" Chris asked. Clara realized she couldn't remember the last time she'd seen someone bleeding. Maybe she *did* have a problem with blood. "Do you want me to do it?"

She looked at Chris. She'd never heard him sound so earnest, so grown up.

"Do you think you can?"

"Ask him if he thinks I can. Look at him," Chris said, nodding toward Gary.

"Gary—" she started.

"I mean, he's a little weird, but that's probably why there's no one I'd trust more with a knife," Gary said.

She turned back to Chris. "Okay, I'm ready."

"Already done," Chris said, pulling the bloody knife away from her thumb.

It took her a moment to register that she was already bleeding. "Look up, look up," Chris said, and she kept her eyes on Gary while he held her hand directly over the skull and squeezed out one, two, three drops of blood. By the time she did look at her hand, Chris had already wrapped a Band-Aid around her thumb.

"Where did you *get* that?" she asked.

"Pockets are important!" he said, returning the bandage's wrapper to one of his pants pockets.

"The page," Gary said. "We need to burn the page with the spell on it. Do you have more matches?"

Chris smiled. "I always have more matches."

Clara took a step toward the backpack and faltered.

"Here, sit down, breathe deep," Chris said.

Am I one of those people who gets woozy at the sight of blood? Am I just now finding this out? Clara thought. She glanced at the skull, with a few rivulets of blood, still wet, working their way down the brow. She felt the color drain from her face. *Yep, I guess I am one of those people.* She sat down cross-legged and breathed deeply.

I still have to get out of here, she thought. *After…*after whatever was about to happen. *The spell will work. It has to!*

Gary fished Book Two out of the backpack's pocket and found the page with the cryptic spell on it. He tore it out and placed it on the skull. The blood glued it in place, with the sigils facing upward.

"Burn it," Clara said. "Do it."

"Time for this quest to end," Chris said, lighting another match and holding it to the corner of the wrinkled paper.

Clara expected it to combust instantly, in some dramatic flash of light. Instead, the flame grew gradually inward from the corner, steadily converting the yellowed paper into black ash. One by one, the symbols on the page disappeared, until there was nothing left but brittle ashes and white smoke.

Clara could hear the buzzing again, and the distant clapping. Where was it coming from?

"Is it done? Does anything else happen? How long do we stay?" Gary voiced what they were all thinking.

The clapping stopped. It was coming from over their heads. Then a new sound, high-pitched and faint, emanated from somewhere above them. It was a song.

"Look!" Chris pointed at the smoke, which was undulating in time to the singing. The smoke formed a spiral, like a slow, sideways tornado, above the skull of Constance Love.

"I farewell take, and pleasure I forsake—"

The three of them stood so still they could hear the faint singing from above form words. The pitch was high, although the melody was as slow as a dirge.

"No torment shall accrue to me—"

"What is that?" Gary asked.

Clara's eyes grew wide. "It's the recitation! Tonight. We must be under the museum's auditorium."

"Oh ye disbelief's children—"

Clara tried to remember what she'd read about the program. "It's the grade schoolers," she said, "from around the county. Singing songs by early Biskopskulla settlers."

"I shall at thine destruction smile—"

"The smoke seems to like the song," Chris said. "As if it's part of the spell."

"For someday I shall return to thee."

"Of course!" Clara realized. "Constance must have known this song would be performed in this exact place at this time. The song…it's an incantation!" She tried to stand, but she still felt a little dizzy.

"Does that mean—maybe Constance *wrote* this song?" asked Gary.

The voices grew in the final crescendo.

"Soon, I shall return to thee."

The spiral glowed brightly, and each one of them decided it was safest to look away. The bright white light cast extraordinarily long shadows that reached out toward the edges of the room.

In the corner along the wall opposite the door, a shadow moved toward them. They weren't alone.

It was a bird. Even without seeing it up close, Gary was certain it was the raven that had startled him in the social studies classroom.

From the floor where she was sitting, Clara could see the doorway to the basement chamber. A moment ago, faint light was shining in. Now, something blocked the light.

The raven did not fly, but walked toward them. As it walked, the space occupied by the bird seemed to grow larger, even as the bird stayed the same size. By the time it had covered half the distance between the room's corner and the altar, it was no longer a bird, but something not quite distinguishable. By the time it reached them, it was a woman. Her skin had the weathered roughness of someone who spent years outdoors, but it was shockingly pale, as if she hadn't been in the sun in a very long time.

Her clothing was as strange as her countenance. She wore what appeared to be a floor-length black coat, made entirely of torn strips of fabric. Her arms were bare from her hands to her elbows.

She produced a green clay bottle from within her garment. She looked from the glowing portal of smoke to Gary to Chris, then back to the smoke. She appeared to be talking to herself. Gary wasn't sure if he should approach her and talk to her, or run.

The smoke stopped moving. A single ring of smoke hovered in the air, still glowing.

"At last," the woman said, her voice a breathy croak. Still holding the bottle, she reached into the smoke ring. Her hand did not come out the other side. She looked from Gary to Chris and her eyes settled on Chris.

Is this what was supposed to happen? wondered Gary.

She looks exactly like I'd expect a witch to look, thought Chris.

She withdrew the bottle from the smoke portal. Her eyes widened. "Constance Love!" she intoned in a voice raspy from disuse. She looked up in many directions, as if talking to fireflies. "I call upon thee, Constance Love! I am your servant, and you in your great wisdom are my preceptor! I entreat your essence, through the great morass of time, come now to this moment! I shall transfer your spirit into your only great-great-great-granddaughter, and the new age shall begin!"

Clara, still on the ground, felt a chill and tried to scoot backward.

With surprising speed, the raven woman leapt onto the altar and poured the contents of the clay bottle onto Chris's head.

"What the—?" Gary exclaimed. But his voice was drowned out by the sound of Chris, screaming and screaming. Chris stumbled, then fell forward through the rapidly dissipating smoke, planting face first in the bones on the table. He continued screaming, pausing only to gasp for air.

Thoroughly alarmed, Clara tried to stand.

Abruptly Chris stopped. He straightened up, threw his shoulders back, and held his hands in front of his face. He looked at the woman in black and smiled a strange, sick smile as he beckoned to her. With surprising strength, she jumped off the altar to stand next to Chris.

"You okay?" Gary said, but as he took a step toward Chris the woman in black hissed at him savagely.

Chris shook his long hair out of his eyes and looked at the woman in black. "Jennifer," he said. He didn't sound like himself. It sounded like several voices talking in unison; Chris's voice could be heard, and a higher-pitched shrill intonation, but also a deep and spidery whisper. "How well you have prepared for this moment, my dear."

Chris looked at Gary. "The...boy. You must have so many questions. Fear not; all will be answered in time."

The music above them had stopped. For a moment there was silence as Gary struggled to take everything in; then—from far above—he heard a new song begin.

Just then Chris noticed Clara getting to her feet behind Gary, and his expression changed to one of abject horror.

"This cannot be!" he shouted. He looked at the woman in black. "What have you done?"

He held his hands in front of his face again and looked at them with disgust. His feet began to twitch, then his legs began to convulse. The shaking seemed to work its way up his body from the floor, until his arms were vibrating so much that he couldn't hold up his hands. He opened his mouth and let out a low, crackling growl.

"No! You fool!" Chris said. "This is not the girl of my blood! I CAN ONLY SURVIVE INSIDE THE GIRL!"

The woman in the black coat—*Oh my gosh*, thought Clara, *is that Jennifer Fahren?*—stepped aside. Clara ran to Chris and grabbed him by the shoulders, attempting to steady him.

"Fix it! Now!" Chris's voices screamed.

Jennifer tried to pour liquid from the green bottle onto Clara, but nothing came out. Chris started foaming at the mouth. The woman jerked the clay bottle in Clara's direction, frantically trying to get the last drops to come out. Then, in frustration, she lifted the bottle above her head.

Before anyone could stop her, she swung her arm in a

downward arc and smashed the bottle on Clara's head. Clara collapsed. Gary, who had his hands in Chris's armpits, trying to hold him up, reached out his arm to slow Clara's fall.

Bright green lightning crackled from Chris to Clara. Gary was so startled he almost let go of them both. The woman in black took a step back.

Chris came to his senses, bracing his hands on his knees and spitting the foam out of his mouth as if he'd tasted something horrendous. Clara's knees buckled, but she caught herself with her hands before her head hit the floor. She pulled herself into a seated position, and then studied her right hand in front of her face, moving one finger at a time.

"If I'm not mistaken," Clara said, in a voice that sounded like Clara's, but was more clipped and formal, "we are a few moments behind schedule. In that case, you'd better step forward, Thaddeus. You know you cannot sneak up on *me*."

From the shadows near the door, a figure emerged. To the people in the room, he was known as Tad Trumpeter, or Theodore Herald, but his original name was Thaddeus Clarion.

"You actually pulled the miracle off," Thaddeus said. "Truly astonishing, Constance. But what's to become of the girl?"

Chris, who had been silent and disoriented, shook himself wearily. "That's not Clara!" he said, turning his head to Gary, but looking at Thaddeus. "She's possessed."

"What a pretty creature you are," Clara/Constance said to Chris. "How odd that I could never see you clearly before."

"She was inside my head," Chris said. "I couldn't move my own body, but I could feel everything she was thinking. She's been lying to us, Gary, this whole time. *She's* the cataclysm. *Constance is the cataclysm.*"

40

Clara seemed taken by surprise, but she quickly recovered and smiled strangely at the boys.

"Oh, you needn't worry. I'm Clara, and I'm fine. I was just out of sorts. What a blunderbuss I've been!"

Gary shook his head as if determining whether his friends were possessed was a thing he did every day. "Okay, that's not convincing at all. You are definitely not Clara."

Clara shouted at Jennifer, "Everything is in place, it must be done!"

Jennifer produced a long slender dagger from somewhere in the fold of her cloak. She brandished it in front of Clara, who shakily stood and faced her, expressionless. The older woman, on the other hand, looked enraptured. She looked like a lifelong fan-club member finally meeting the celebrity of her dreams.

Jennifer turned to face Thaddeus, positioning herself between him and Clara, as if to protect her. Then, abruptly, she ran out of the room, carving a circular path toward the only doorway.

Clara looked Thaddeus up and down.

"I did say," she said in the formal voice, "that I would see you again."

"This enchantment is an abomination, Constance."

"The spell has worked, Thaddeus. You never believed the spell would work."

"Your soul will not remain in that body. Of what use is it to revisit a few moments on this earth, after all these years?"

"A soul can remain in a body if a powerful witch prevents its departure," Clara/Constance told him. "A powerful witch who has kept his own soul in his own body for hundreds of years. A man such as you, Thaddeus."

"I cannot do that, Constance. Too many will suffer if you return to this world. You showed me that."

Gary interrupted, "What did you do to Clara?"

Constance, in Clara's body, did not take her eyes off Thaddeus. "She is still here. The girl. I can hear her inside this body." She chuckled. "The dear girl. Dear, dear girl. You have served your purpose."

"You are mad, Constance," said Thaddeus. "And your soul will soon slip from this body into the ether again, where you can do no harm."

"This child," spat Constance, "is the daughter's daughter of our daughter's daughter. She is my flesh and blood. And yours, Thaddeus."

"Leave the child be," Thaddeus said, "The world has changed. The village has changed. Everyone who ever wronged you is dead and gone."

"Except you."

The woman, Jennifer Fahren, appeared in the doorway again, holding a familiar-looking thin green candle in one hand, and what looked to be a bunch of candles in the other.

Clara/Constance looked approvingly at her.

"Stop her!" Chris found the strength to shout, his voice weak. "She's going to seal us in! With dynamite!"

Gary felt like slapping his own forehead. "The boxes in the hallway! HCD! Hawley Charles Douglas! His whole stockpile is down here. She'll turn this place into a tomb!"

"She's going to sacrifice herself," Chris said, "all to try to get Constance resurrected. If the doorway collapses, Gary, you and I could die in a couple of weeks, but Tad could get trapped down here for a hundred years."

"This plan is sick," Gary said.

"Constance has trouble predicting what Tad will do, so she had to figure out a lot of options."

Clara/Constance steadied herself against the altar. "I'm growing weaker, Thaddeus, but if you make my transition into this body permanent, I know an enchantment that will allow us both to escape harm. If I die…then all who are present will die."

Somehow, Jennifer lit the candle with a flourish. Gary and Tad discovered, simultaneously, that their feet were frozen to the ground. Neither could move to stop her.

Jennifer positioned herself directly under the door frame. If the dynamite went off there, it could create a cave-in that would block off the room's only exit. She did not speak, but she continued to smile and gaze eerily at the four individuals in the center of the basement room.

Then she lit the fuse of the dynamite.

For a moment it seemed like the old jute cord wouldn't catch. Then, with a hiss, it lit up like a sparkler.

Slowly the flame moved along the fuse toward the blasting cap inside the dynamite. The boys shouted at Jennifer to stop, to save herself, but she just looked at them with a beatific expression.

Then she crumpled to the floor.

Behind her stood Regina Farber, holding an electric cattle prod.

A few things happened next in quick succession: Regina shocked Jennifer one more time, for good measure, at which point the younger woman hissed and her body folded in on itself, becoming a raven and fluttering away. Regina walked with her cane to the place where the dynamite had fallen and stepped on the fuse with a low-heel, closed-toe pump.

"I knew this would come in handy one day," she said, brandishing the cattle prod at the raven.

Gary and Thaddeus were able to move again.

Clara began to cry.

Chris spoke with great effort. "It's not over. Constance figured out a spell to transfer her soul out of her body right before she died. She needed a blood relative to be the receptacle. That's why it had to be Clara, not me."

"This is messed up," Gary said.

"It's worse than that," Chris said. "*Much* worse. Her soul

has been frozen for 140 years. That's powerful magic. She can't just come back. She needed a sacrifice."

Gary tried to keep his eyes on both the raven and Clara. "One of us?"

"More than that. It's everyone. Everyone in the auditorium upstairs. A hundred and forty people. One person for every year she was gone. It was all part of the spell."

"What?" Gary said. "When?"

"The song—the children singing—it's not just an incantation—it's a sacrifice. They're all dying. When the spell is finished, they'll be gone."

"It's already happening," Chris said. "Listen…the music is slowing down. She was counting on Thaddeus not knowing about the sacrifice…until it was too late." He looked at Thaddeus. "Help."

Thaddeus began whispering quickly and deliberately, in a language the young people present could not understand.

"He's going to try to expunge me, to cast me out into the ether," Clara/Constance said to the raven. "There's only one thing to do." Her eyes widened. "Do it."

Jennifer Fahren materialized beside Clara, holding the long dagger, and before anyone knew what was happening, she stabbed Clara Hutchins in the chest.

In the split-second before she collapsed, Clara herself found the breath to scream.

41

Constance Love said not a word as she was carried bodily from the shed miles away toward the copse of trees deep in the woods on the edge of the colony. The brothers Spencer and old Mr. Kronberg tied her hands and covered her head with a cloth sack.

It didn't matter; she already knew where they were taking her. She knew many, many things.

A circle of colonists had gathered. While not every individual was present, Constance was surprised how many had come to her trial. Mary and Carl Olofsson were not there; surely some men had been dispatched to keep them detained in their house.

Constance had foreseen her own death, and she had known for a long time that it was inevitable. But she had also foreseen a way to cheat death, if the right conditions were met. It took years to complete the preparations for her plan: to gather the withered broom straw from Mr. Kronberg's field; to steal the head of the unborn baby Carson; to eat the heart of the girl from Altona.

What wisdom she had gained in the process!

With each transgression, Constance lost a little more of her soul. And, truth be told, it became harder for her to maintain the mask of a decent, God-fearing woman. Only her sister and brother-in-law, sweet Mary and Carl, were blind to the wickedness that shone behind her eyes.

Constance could see into the future, but her vision wasn't perfected. Her sight was blurred, as it were, the more human lives intersected around a place, or an object, or an event. An object that remained untouched, however, gave her a clear pinhole view of the events surrounding its discovery.

Constance had realized that she would need acolytes, individuals in the distant future who would put the final stages of her spell into motion. Initially she thought she could reach out, via writing, to a vulnerable young girl and provide her with a whole new life—give her instructions, yes, but also introduce her to a whole new belief system, a private religion based in a special magical book.

At one point, Constance believed she could manipulate this girl to do anything she wanted. Constance wrote page after page of directives; she could persuade the girl to leave her family, to live in solitude, to practice magic in a secret basement sanctuary until she mastered the art of transforming her body into that of a raven.

As Constance wrote, each new paragraph altered the outcome of the future she was viewing. At first she would write a page, or a paragraph, and then use her gift to view the future that page would inspire. As she developed her abilities, she found that she could envision alternate futures simply by *deciding* to write a paragraph. If she needed to adjust the course of events, she could change her mind and decide to write something different.

Then she hit a snag. On the date of her spell's completion, some one hundred forty years hence, there would be no living descendant in Biskopskulla. Catherine Hutchins, an elderly widow by this time, was fated to die a few weeks before the winter solstice. This meant there would be no one in Biskopskulla with Constance Love's blood, the crucial ingredient in the spell. The solution came to Constance in a dream: if Catherine Hutchins died earlier, during the summer, then two more of Constance's bloodline would return to Biskopskulla. All it would take is a little help from a raven flying in through a broken window.

As she wrote the directive that would make that come to pass, Constance saw a clearer picture of the girl who would come to live in the house Carl Olofsson had built on Park Street and Mattsson Street.

She was a strong-willed girl, and clever. She would be able to solve the problems leading up to the solstice, and when the time came to transfer Constance's soul across the decades, she would be a far more fitting vessel than her grandmother could ever have been.

The final weeks of Constance's life were devoted to leaving the clues that would guide this girl, Clara, toward her new destiny.

At the clearing, the trial of Constance Love was about to begin.

One of the village trustees, Jonas Swanson, sat as judge, while another Jonas, Mr. Jacobson, interrogated the witnesses against her. Constance paid them no heed, and she let her mind wander as Mrs. Carlson sobbed and Margaret Allgren's eyes betrayed a gleeful bloodlust.

Constance thought back to her final argument with Thaddeus.

"I shall never understand," he had said, "how you can have such little regard for your fellow human beings."

"*Are* they my fellows, though, really? The people of Biskopskulla have wronged me, and they will murder me someday."

"If you know this to be true, then leave. You can live a long and happy life."

"A life as long as yours?"

"It is not my place to grant immortality to others; the price is too great."

"I have seen a time where witches are an afterthought, a disregarded superstition. Where technology is magic. It is *there* that I shall live my long and happy life."

"I cannot allow you to undertake this enchantment. Neither to enact it nor to endure it."

"Then stop them, Thaddeus. Risk your own life and persuade them not to try me for the crime of witchcraft, else this will all be your fault."

Whether she meant it was unimportant. It was what she needed to say to ensure that he would return, that he would be present on that future solstice when the spell was completed.

Thaddeus, her mentor, had become just another ingredient in her plan.

Beliefs about witches abounded in the community. Some believed they floated in water. Others believed they sank. Some believed a witch would always confess in the right circumstances. Others believed a witch would always lie.

No one remembered exactly where the legend of the stone originated. Some believed Erik Mattsson himself had decreed that the large, strangely shaped stone jutting out of the ground had the capacity to detect magic. Others knew this was impossible, that Mattsson had no knowledge of the hidden world, that the stone hadn't even been surveyed until after his death. It was as if the stone itself had implanted its existence in the minds of the village. One day, everyone knew something they hadn't known the day before.

Certainly, no one had witnessed the stone's power. No one present could have confidently predicted what would happen when Constance Love, at the end of her trial, was lowered onto the slab of rock. So it was with considerable astonishment that the gathered crowd watched the great coffin-shaped stone light up, not like a fire but like an ember, with yellow light so bright it became white and hurt their eyes.

"Guilty!" Jonas Swanson's voice carried far on the still night. Cries of "guilty" filled the air as the gathered crowd repeated the verdict. In no time at all, a noose was produced and thrown over a strong branch of the white oak tree.

Constance was lifted up onto a stool—she did not resist. The noose was placed over her neck.

"Have you any last words?" Trustee Swanson asked.

"I will return to see you moldering in the ground. Your

children's children's children will suffer because of what you do today."

Trustee Swanson gulped but did not reply. Later he would form a committee to ensure that Constance's body was buried properly and securely in the dead of night, close to the people she might wish not to harm, and all present would swear never to reveal its location.

Constance tried not to turn her head, so as not to reveal by its sound the thin piece of paper she had sewn into the collar of her shirt.

She stood stock-still on the stool. In spite of it all, she was afraid of death, though she had less reason to be so than almost anyone in the world. Almost.

The murmuring crowd grew silent, and she knew the time was near.

She didn't look to see who kicked the stool out from under her. It didn't matter. They were all guilty.

As she fell, the noose tightened around her neck and the rope rubbed violently against her collar. The paper, with its carefully inscribed sigils, was ripped apart, beginning an elaborate spell that would take nearly a century and a half to complete.

The last thing Constance thought was, *It begins.*

42

Regina Farber had no medical training, but she knew the wound was serious. The girl who had screamed grew silent, as the blood on her shirt spread alarmingly fast.

The taller boy, with dark hair, rushed to her and held her. The woman in black, who moments ago had seemed almost superhuman in her strength and agility, sank to the floor. She reached out to stop the boy, to prevent him from reaching the girl, and the other boy—the one with long blond hair— grabbed her arm and bit her, hard.

"Save me, Thaddeus. Bind me to this body along with the girl. Keep me on this world with you," the girl said. Her voice was weak.

He spoke gently, compassionately. "It's true I can prevent death by enchanting the body to retain its soul. But I cannot save you now, knowing the true cost. I'm so sorry for what you have become. You will die, Constance, for a second time."

The girl swayed, her eyes focusing beyond the dirty room, into something no one else present could see. "I see nothing," she said. "I see...everything. I can see...eternity!" Her eyes betrayed a look of recognition. A look of remembrance. A final look of realization.

Then her head rolled to the side and she collapsed.

"No!" the dark-haired boy yelled. He placed a hand on the wound in the girl's chest and pressed against it. "Direct pressure," he said to himself. "Apply direct pressure."

"It is too late, Gary," the man said softly.

"No!" the boy repeated. The other boy was crying. He took off his jacket and placed it on the girl's legs like a blanket. She lay motionless.

43

For a moment, there was silence.

Then there was a small movement under the girl's collar. A glint of gold caught the shaky overhead light.

"What the—?" the blond boy said.

With surprising strength, the man reached around both boys and lifted them bodily off the ground, then stepped backward, away from the girl, his eyes wide with surprise.

"That talisman," he said with reverence, "is very powerful."

Regina knew that what she was seeing was impossible. A tiny golden insect—a butterfly, or perhaps a moth—had crawled with purpose out of the girl's shirt and was marching, with tiny metallic legs, above the knife wound, kneading the fabric like a cat about to sleep. It fluttered its wings and then reached its front legs into the injury, then *wiggled underneath the girl's flesh.*

It was unmistakable—one instant the golden insect was there, and the next it had disappeared within the body of the girl.

Regina, who had been a speechless witness for the past few minutes, broke the silence.

"What is happening?" she asked of no one in particular.

"The moth charm brings luck," the dark-haired boy said quietly. "Wards off diseases of the eye. On rare occasions, it can even mend...a broken...heart."

For another instant they all watched, motionless.

Then the moth emerged from the girl's chest, climbed up toward her throat, clasped onto the string around her neck, and froze.

Silence.

The girl coughed. Slowly, she opened her eyes.

44

Clara opened her eyes. She was in bed. It wasn't her own bed; this bed was slender and the sheets were pulled far too taut across the mattress. It was a hospital room. She tried to move, but a pain in her chest forced her to reconsider.

"Clara?" Her mother woke up from the chair where she'd been dozing. "Clara, honey? How do you feel?"

"Hi, Mom," Clara said, her voice raspy. "Could I get some water?" She thought back to the last moments she remembered—the green lightning in the museum basement. "Please," she added, before closing her eyes again.

The next day Clara was feeling well enough to sit up. Her mother sat by her bed, talking to her slowly and holding her hand. Her mother was under the impression, Clara found out later, that the woman who had attacked Clara was a psychotic member of a religious cult. Gary's talent for lying had no doubt helped shape this narrative, but the presence of two adult witnesses at the scene couldn't have hurt. Three days had passed since the incident. The nurses told her that she had suffered a traumatic wound, but that the blade that cut her had somehow managed to avoid damaging her heart.

"It's amazing," one nurse said. "Magical—a miracle!" After lunch, of which Clara had only managed to eat some grapes and a few chunks of cantaloupe, the same nurse said, "You have some friends who have been coming and sitting in the waiting room every day. Should I tell them they can see you this afternoon?"

Clara was alone, watching a daytime talk show, when they came in: Gary, followed by Chris, and...

"Tad?" she exclaimed.

"Call me Thaddeus," he said.

The boys hovered uncertainly for a moment, until Clara said, "You can't hug me yet, my stitches might rip." Then they both sat down. Thaddeus leaned against the wall, his hands clasped before him.

"You've missed a lot of long, boring explanations," Gary said with a grin, before launching into a long explanation of his own. Chris interjected where appropriate, but Thaddeus remained quiet and let the boys do the talking.

"Obviously, we didn't have all the information when we set about our quest," Gary said, and Chris exhaled as a way of saying *That was an understatement.* "Constance was right that Thaddeus was trying to stop her. But what she didn't tell us was that she was trying to kill everyone in town and possess your body for all eternity."

The Spell of Protection for which Constance had so carefully provided instructions was, in fact, a Spell of Resurrection. The final ingredient had been Clara herself, the blood relative and the youngest remaining descendant of the witch trying to bring herself back from the dead.

"So we thought he was the bad guy," Chris said, gesturing toward Thaddeus, "but he thought *we* were the bad guys. Otherwise, we could have teamed up. But Constance had already led at least one kid to the dark side, and I guess he thought that was a real possibility with us too."

"Jennifer Fahren was recruited by Constance to be her acolyte. She communicated with her by hiding a book," Gary said, "which was kind of her MO, you know? Jenny found the book about 110 years after Constance put it there."

"That's crazy," Clara said. "I can't believe someone would spend their whole life devoted to something they read in a book when they were a teenager."

"I dunno. You hear stories all the time about high school kids who start reading message boards in their bedrooms and turn into neo-Nazis," Chris said. "It's not impossible."

"Her plan would have totally worked," Gary smirked, "if the acolyte hadn't mistaken Chris for a girl and transferred Constance's spirit into him first."

"I always thought people were *kidding* about my beautiful hair and amazing cheekbones," Chris said. "I got so much flak, and here I end up saving the town. I was actually even thinking about cutting my hair next year—"

"—but now your hair is like a superhero!" Gary interrupted.

"Basically, yeah," Chris said. "With great hair comes great responsibility."

"The acolyte," Clara said, "Jennifer. Where is she now?"

"Tad has her," Gary said. Then, noticing Thaddeus's scowl, he added, "I mean, Thaddeus does. She's a raven now and doesn't seem to be able to turn back into a human, so he's taking care of her for now."

"Her mom said she vanished into the air. But that's literally how it happened," Chris said.

Clara looked over at Thaddeus, who remained quiet. He smiled at her. She still found his expression reptilian, but today he looked like a slightly more pleasant reptile.

"Oh, wait; does she know?" Chris asked Gary.

Clara guessed immediately what he was talking about.

"You're my...great-great-great-grandfather?" she said to Thaddeus.

"Indeed I am," he said. "It's incontrovertible. Constance took great pains to hide her child—our child—from me. I heard rumors, of course, over the decades, but I convinced myself it was rubbish."

"It's nice to meet you officially," Clara said.

"The pleasure is truly all mine," said Thaddeus.

"So, you and Constance...dated?"

"We had a courtship," Thaddeus said.

"Was she always...was she ever...I don't know..."

"Constance was intelligent, and talented, and very charismatic. But, over time, I realized that she was something else too. I believe she was what we now call a psychopath."

"That must have been a rough thing to realize."

"I lacked maturity then. It was a hundred and forty-two years ago." Thaddeus looked almost sheepish.

There was an awkward pause. Chris broke the silence.

"Oh, and that lady—the woman with the cattle prod! She was pretty cool, wasn't she?"

"Yeah," agreed Clara. "She was something else."

"Her name is Regina Farber. And from what I gather, she too had been influenced by Constance," said Thaddeus. "In her case, unwittingly. I have spoken to her. I think she is trustworthy."

Clara repositioned herself in the hospital bed. "Are you going to tell us not to tell anyone what we've been through?"

Thaddeus's bicolored eyes twinkled. "I suspect I don't need to tell you that, do I? Nevertheless, I shall." He became serious. "There are witches in every corner of the globe, and there have been for millennia. One constant has been this: Whenever plain folk discover, as a society, that there are witches among them, death follows. Witch hunts are a consistent feature of history, and they are brutal, both for the witches and for the men and women swept up with them. Do you know—do any of you know—when the last witch execution on Earth occurred?"

Clara looked from Gary to Chris.

"Was there one after Constance? In the 1800s?"

"The last witch to face trial and execution did so yesterday morning, in Papua New Guinea," Thaddeus said solemnly. "Tomorrow will surely see the murder, elsewhere in the world, of a different witch. Or at least a woman or man who looks like a witch."

"Because of this ongoing threat of persecution," Thaddeus continued, "modern witches are very, very protective of the secrecy surrounding our existence. You might think that modern America is different, that witches could come forward and demonstrate their gifts and live out their lives in peace, but history has proven that notion to be folly. When a person tries to go public with evidence of witchcraft, if it's real witchcraft, there are those in the community of witches who find ways to make the evidence—or the person—disappear."

"Did someone in the witch community kill Raymond Bergstrom?" Gary asked.

"No, although in fact Raymond Bergstrom *was* a member of the witch community, at least in a manner of speaking. He wasn't particularly skilled, and he had few friends, but he could divine the occasional future event. Mental illness is not unique to plain folk, but it can be particularly dangerous in a witch. I believe the acolyte Jennifer Fahren determined that Mr. Bergstrom was trying to interfere with Constance's plan and she dispatched him of her own volition. She, however, is incapable of speech at the moment."

Clara remembered something. "What about all those towns you were at where tragedies happened? Deer Grove? Fort Monroe? Bardtown?"

Thaddeus looked surprised. "I didn't realize you were aware of those. Constance must have grown truly powerful indeed toward the end of her days." His face became even more solemn than usual. "In recent years, I have devoted my time to preventing unnatural tragedies. There has been an uptick in violence created by witches. Those towns you named…those were the places I've failed."

He looked so sad that Clara found herself wanting to provide comfort. "At least you succeeded in Biskopskulla."

"Yes. I suppose for the most part I did."

Clara repositioned herself and winced.

"We've busied you for too long," Thaddeus said. "Dear girl—"

"Please don't call me that!"

"Of course. Clara. I think it's time these young gentlemen and I took our leave." He stepped away from the wall to stand at Clara's bedside.

"Clara, if you'll indulge me," Thaddeus said, "I'd like to show you something outside your window. Can you see the buildings across the street?"

Clara turned her head to face the large window on the northern wall of the hospital room. Thaddeus pointed with his left hand, directing her attention to some offices outside.

With his right hand, Thaddeus slapped her, hard.

At least that's what he tried to do. Before he could make contact with Clara's face, her hand shot up from the mattress with alarming speed and forcefully gripped his wrist.

"Dude, what are you doing?" asked Chris.

"I'm...sorry," Clara said, unsure what was going on. "I'm not sure why I did that."

"I suspected this might be the case," Thaddeus said. "Constance's ability to prognosticate was stronger when she faced immediate danger. You predicted—unconsciously, perhaps—that I was about to strike you."

"Clara," Gary asked, "do you remember the name of our scholastic bowl coach? Do you remember how fast you ran the Hawley Douglas 5K race?"

"Mrs. Maynard is our coach, and I don't remember my time, because I don't care."

"Okay, she's definitely the real Clara," Gary said.

Clara looked worried.

"Yes, of course it's Clara," Thaddeus said. "Don't worry, Clara. You're not possessed. I would know it if you were. Constance Love is dead. But it may be the case that some part of her remains and is trapped in your subconscious."

"How do I get rid of it?"

"That is an interesting question that will require some study. For the time being, you should rest and heal. For my part, I think I shall remain in Biskopskulla for a while longer.

Perhaps I can even get to know my great-great grandchild and you. It has been a long, long time since I have had any family."

"Are you going to come clean with Clara's mom?" Chris asked.

"No, I don't think the time is right for that yet. But I think your school will be needing a new history teacher very soon, and my application will be impeccable."

"Whoa," Gary said. "That sounds a little ominous, Thaddeus."

"Don't worry, children. I'm not one of the evil witches."

Later that day, Clara's mother stopped in with some flowers and a comically oversized greeting card.

"Mom!" Clara rolled her eyes. "You didn't have to get me flowers."

"These aren't from me. A girl from your school stopped by the house today with these."

Clara opened the card. The inside was covered with messages from her classmates.

Kaitlyn had written: "CLARA!!! I'M SO GLAD YOU'RE OKAY! YOU HAD US ALL ON TENTERHOOKS! I CAN'T WAIT TO SEE YOU AGAIN!"

Myron had written: "Clara, you are stronger than Dracula." (Clara realized he was making a joke about being staked in the heart.) "Get well soon."

Edison thanked her for making him feel welcome in the United States and told her if she missed any of the spring semester, she'd have to come visit Ecuador next year to make up for it.

There were dozens of signatures from people who weren't on the scholastic bowl team. Mrs. Maynard wrote a nice note, as did Mr. Hawthorne and Mr. Froehlich, and even some teachers Clara had never met.

As she read the card, she remembered that school was not

yet back in session. That meant someone had taken this card from door to door, getting signatures, just to make Clara feel better.

She'd been a little preoccupied during her time here, but maybe this town wasn't as unpleasant as she'd originally feared. Maybe Biskopskulla had potential after all.

A week later, Mr. Froehlich learned that a cache of stock certificates his father had purchased in the eighties was being held by the state's unclaimed property division. One of the companies his father had invested in had merged with a major telecommunications firm in the nineties, and the stock was now worth over a hundred thousand dollars. Although it wasn't enough to retire on, the windfall meant that Mr. Froehlich could pursue his dream of going to graduate school.

He applied and was accepted to the history program at Boyd University. The school board advertised in print and online for a qualified replacement, but three savvy young Prairie Dale students suspected that a few resumés might get lost in the mail.

Clara was released from the hospital after a few more days. The first night back home, her mother wouldn't let her out of her sight, and Clara realized that in some sense they would both need to go through a period of recovery, but that their relationship would get back to normal one day. She could see that day quite clearly.

One night not long after, snow fell and blanketed the town of Biskopskulla.

In the house at the corner of Park and Mattsson, a girl and her mother slept, secure in the knowledge that for the time being, they had a safe home, and a happy one.

In the early morning hours before the township snowplows cleared the roads, every surface was covered in a downy white coat: every rooftop, every street, every highway, even the graves in the cemetery. With most of the cars and paved roads obscured, many parts of the historic town looked exactly as they had appeared more than a century earlier, when the European settlers who founded Biskopskulla were still alive, raising their families, adapting their beliefs, and trying to survive in this brave, strange, sometimes beautiful new world.

Then, while the morning wore on, the ringing of cell phones and the roar of snowblowers broke the silence. Footprints and tire tracks cut through the snow. Students trudged on snowy sidewalks in brightly colored synthetic jackets, tiny audio speakers in their ears. The illusion of timelessness was shattered. The present, as it always does, overwrote the past.

ACKNOWLEDGMENTS

Like many writers, I have benefited from the guidance of a number of wonderful teachers, from kindergarten through graduate school. A special shout-out is due to Mr. Marty Golby, my high school English teacher and forensics coach, whose poetic respect for the small towns of Illinois, once inscrutable to me, has left a lasting impression.

I owe a heap of gratitude to many colleagues and friends, especially my patient and helpful early readers, August Benassi III and Grahm Eberhardt, and to my indefatigable editor, Jaynie Royal, and the team at Regal House/Fitzroy. To my parents, for encouraging a love of reading and giving me space to try things out. To John, for being my rock, and to our dog Koko and our late dog Oso, whose ghost, we are certain, remains vigilant.